The Mormon Image in Literature

The Mormon Image in Literature reprints important literary works by and about Mormons—from the sensational anti-polygamy books and dime novels of the Civil War era to the first attempts of Mormon writers to craft a regional literature in their Great Basin kingdom. Each volume contains a critical introduction, helpful annotations, and multiple appendices that enlighten and enliven the text. These volumes have been designed for both Mormon and non-Mormon readers who want to understand the cultural importance of Mormonism during the first Latter-day Saint century.

BOADICEA;

THE MORMON WIFE.

LIFE-SCENES IN UTAH.

Beautifully Illustrated.

EDITED BY

ALFREDA EVA BELL.

Published by

ARTHUR R. ORTON,

BALTIMORE, PHILADELPHIA, NEW YORK, AND BUFFALO.

[ORIGINAL COPYRIGHT PAGE]

BOADICEA;

THE MORMON WIFE

LIFE-SCENES IN UTAH

edited by

Alfreda Eva Bell

1855

Edited and Annotated by
Michael Austin
and Ardis E. Parshall

SALT LAKE CITY, 2016
GREG KOFFORD BOOKS

ISBN 978-1-58958-566-9 (paperback)
Also available in ebook.

Greg Kofford Books
P.O. Box 1362
Draper, UT 84020
www.gregkofford.com

2020   19   18   17   16   5   4   3   2   1

Library of Congress Control Number: 2016939906

CONTENTS.

CHAPTER IX.

CHAPTER X.

CHAPTER XI.

CHAPTER XII.

CHAPTER XIII.

CHAPTER XIV.

CHAPTER XV.

CHAPTER XVI.

CHAPTER XVII.

CHAPTER XVIII.

CHAPTER XIX.

CHAPTER XX.

CHAPTER XXI.

CHAPTER XXII.

CHAPTER XXIII.

CHAPTER XXIV.

CHAPTER XXV.

CHAPTER XXVI.

CHAPTER XXVII.

CHAPTER XXVIII.

CHAPTER XXIX.

CHAPTER XXX.

CHAPTER XXXI.

CHAPTER XXXII.

CHAPTER XXXIII.

CHAPTER XXXIV.

CHAPTER XXXV.

CHAPTER XXXVI.

APPENDIX 1.

APPENDIX 2.

Boadicea; the Mormon Wife:
Life-Scenes in Utah

A CRITICAL INTRODUCTION

The nineteenth century's flood of popular fiction about Mormons began in earnest in 1855. Between 1830 and 1854, only three novels published in America or Great Britain even mentioned Mormonism or Mormon characters.[1] Three more appeared in 1855: Alfreda Eva Bell's *Boadicea; the Mormon Wife: Life-Scenes in Utah* (1855); Maria Ward's *Female Life Among the Mormons: A Narrative of Many Years' Personal Experience* (1855); and Orvilla S. Belisle's *The Prophets; or, Mormonism Unveiled* (1855). A fourth—Metta Victoria Fuller Victor's *Mormon Wives*—appeared a few months later in 1856, completing the tetralogy that one scholar now calls "the nucleus of the first wave of propaganda" against Mormon polygamy.[2] By the end of the century, the number would be counted in the hundreds.

All four novels can be loosely characterized as "anti-Mormon" in that all of them express concern for the threat that polygamous Mormons posed to American morals. All four of them lament the plight of Mormon women forced into a life of servitude and debauchery by a corrupt theocratic system. It is no coincidence that all four novels had (or at least pretended to have) female authors—as did most of the subsequent anti-polygamy literature of the nineteenth century. Most Americans saw plural marriage as a form of captivity for women, making it comparable to slavery—the other great evil that crusading writers attacked vociferously in the 1850s. In 1856, the new Republican Party held its first convention

---

1. The first novel to feature Mormon characters was Frederick Marryat's *Monsieur Violet* (London: Dent, 1843), which had its hero encountering Mormons in Nauvoo during a series of travels through the Western United States. The second was John Russell's *The Mormoness; or The Trials of Mary Maverick* (Alton, Ill.: Courier Steam Press, 1853). The third was Robert Richards's (pseud.) *The Californian Crusoe, or, The Lost Treasure Found: A Tale of Mormonism* (London: John Henry Parker, 1854).

2. Sarah Barringer Gordon, *The Mormon Question: Polygamy and Constitutional Conflict in Nineteenth-Century America* (Chapel Hill: University of North Carolina Press, 2002), 29.

in Philadelphia and dedicated itself to eradicating the "twin relics of barbarism": polygamy and slavery.

The connection between the two relics, as legal historian Sarah Barringer Gordon writes, "was deep and abiding in political thought across the North."[3] Much of this was just good politics. Slavery was a thorny issue that divided the country and would soon lead to a catastrophic civil war. Polygamy, on the other hand, was universally despised by all good Christians in both the North and the South. By linking them together, Republicans could use the national outrage over the recent and relatively isolated problem of polygamy to peel away support for the much larger and expansive problem of slavery. This connection was especially galling to Southern Democrats, as Republicans called for federal intervention against polygamy that would undermine the principles of territorial sovereignty—the same principles that those same Democrats relied on to support the institution of slavery. Both sides knew very well that, if one peculiar domestic institution could be attacked by the federal government, then so could the other one. Democrats, therefore, were forced to choose between defending the rights of polygamists or approving federal legislation that they knew would eventually be used to attack slavery.

But the early anti-polygamy novels worried about more than just the fate of a small number of Mormon women in far-off Deseret. In all four of these books, polygamy is presented as a grave threat to the American family because it indulges men's deepest desires and removes the practical restraints that civilized society places on the male libido. "All men have a passion for variety," says one of Maria Ward's characters.[4] All men, therefore, would be polygamists if law and custom allowed it. In all four of the novels, the female protagonist marries a good and decent man who promises monogamy. But, when Mormonism enters the picture, the husband gives into internal and external pressures and takes another wife—only to realize his mistake and repent as either he or his wife succumbs to an unnatural death. The not-so-subtle subtext of these books is that

---

3. Ibid., 55.

4. MariaWard, *Female Life Among the Mormons: A Narrative of Many Years' Personal Experience* (New York: J.C. Derby, 1855), 211.

America will face dire consequences if the entire weight of law and culture are not utilized to confine men to a single sexual partner.

But these books were also written to make a quick buck. Each of them shows signs of hasty writing and outright plagiarism—not to mention ignoring available evidence about Mormon life—in order to capitalize on popular outrage. By most accounts they were wildly successful in doing so. *Female Life Among the Mormons*, for example, reportedly sold 40,000 copies within the first few weeks of publication.[5] These were remarkable sales figures for a mid-nineteenth-century book by an unknown author—sales attributable to the enormous interest that Mormonism occasioned when Americans finally learned that the Saints were openly practicing polygamy.

Even more than the other three novels, though, *Boadicea, the Mormon Wife* appears to have been hastily constructed to take advantage of the surge in popular interest about Mormon polygamy. Unlike the other three books, which were published in traditional book format, *Boadicea* was more like an illustrated pamphlet than a novel. It was printed on cheap newsprint with no cover, with the final page advertising another tawdry "true" story for the low price of 15 cents. And though the book ended with page 97, it was actually only 82 pages, but began on page 15 rather than 1—a deliberate strategy that the authors of low-end books used to make their wares appear more substantial. We do not know how many books like this were published in the 1850s. They were not designed for long shelf lives, and the few that do remain often make references (usually through back page advertisements) to others that have been lost. They seem to have occupied the cultural space that dime novels would occupy in the next decade and that comic books would occupy in the next century: low-concept, low production value stories written quickly and sold cheaply to the newly literate masses.

WHO WAS "ALFREDA EVA BELL"?

False pagination is not the only deception that *Boadicea* perpetrates on its readers. The person listed as the editor, "Alfreda Eva

---

5. Leonard J. Arrington and Jon Haupt, "Intolerable Zion: The Image of Mormonism in Nineteenth-Century American Literature," *Western Humanities Review* 22 (Summer 1968): 253.

Bell," is also a part of the fiction. No person of this name can be found in any of the records of the day, and the only other work credited to the same author is an 1864 book titled, *The Rebel Cousins, or, Life and Love in Secessia*—an anti-Confederacy book published towards the end of the Civil War. That Bell is a character in the latter story rather than an actual author can be seen in the book's elaborate subtitle: *The Autobiography of the Beautiful Bertha Stephens, the Accomplished Niece of the Hon. Alexander Hamilton Stephens, Vice-President of the Southern Confederacy ... Written by Herself, and Prepared for Publication by her Friend, Alfreda Eva Bell.* Alexander Hamilton Stephens was indeed the vice president of the Confederacy, but he did not have a niece named Bertha, accomplished or otherwise—a fact which strongly suggests that "her Friend, Alfreda Eva Bell" is equally fictional. We see this even more clearly in *Boadicea; the Mormon Wife*, which is listed as "edited by" and not "written by" Alfreda Eva Bell. Only the first two chapters are even putatively presented as the work of an author; the rest consists of sections from Boadicea's journal selected by the editor. This is a role much like that given by Miguel Cervantes to the "great Arab historian, Cid Hamete Benengeli—the fictional editor of a fictional narrative created by an author who is claiming (with very little probability) to be simply reporting the truth.

If Alfreda Eva Bell is part of the fiction, then who wrote *Boadicea*? The most likely candidate is Arthur R. Orton, who is listed on the title page as the "publisher." We know that Orton published at least eighteen lurid crime pamphlets between 1851 and 1855, all of them claiming to be true stories, and most of them either published anonymously or attributed to a character in the narrative. Beyond these writings, we have only a few tantalizing clues about his life. Records from a Roman Catholic parish in Philadelphia list an Arthur R. Orton who was born in 1826 and died in 1855, making him twenty-eight or twenty-nine at the time of his death.[6] The date of death is confirmed by a burial record for Arthur R. Orton dated December 29, 1855[7]

6. Historical Society of Pennsylvania; Philadelphia, Pennsylvania; Collection Name: *Historic Pennsylvania Church and Town Records*; Reel: 227.

7. Records of the David H. Bowen Funeral Home in the Historical Society of Pennsylvania; Philadelphia, Pennsylvania; Collection Name: *Historic Pennsylvania Church and Town Records*.

and by a newspaper announcement placed in the Philadelphia *Public Ledger* on January 12, 1856 by the local Odd Fellow lodge of which he was a member.[8] Two other intriguing notices from "A.R. Orton" appear in the *Public Ledger*. In February of 1853, Orton advertised for "Three young MEN, to canvass for something new." In a second, published just three weeks before his death, Orton advertised a new pamphlet called *Terrific Combat in Constantinople* written by "the Russian sisters, Sisbirn and Minie Straetdoff . . . just published at the low price of 15 cents."[9] Though no copy of this pamphlet remains, it is precisely the sort of thing that Orton is known to have written.

The only other thing we know for sure about Orton is that he occasionally collaborated with E(rastus) E(lmer) Barclay (1820–1888), perhaps the nineteenth century's most famous author of lurid pamphlets and pseudo-memoirs. Barclay pioneered many of the narrative and marketing conventions that defined the genre for people like Orton. Nearly all of Barclay's titles inflate their page count, and, in most cases, he claims only editorial credit for the work and assigns authorship to either the protagonist or to a fictional editor who figures in some minor way in the text. And even though Barclay published all of his pamphlets in Philadelphia, his title pages often reflect a place of publication somehow related to the story. Furthermore, Barclay did not sell through bookstores or newsstands; he "hired his own salesmen and gave each an exclusive territory. With a stack of pamphlets and broadside sheets, these agents would go from door to door, leaving the descriptive sheets, returning after a circuit of the street either to pick up the sheets or to sell the pamphlets described."[10] Something like this is certainly what Orton had in mind when he advertised for "Three young MEN, to canvass for something new."

In 1851, Barclay and Orton co-published three sensational pamphlets. At this time, Barclay would have been a seasoned veteran of thirty with ten years of experience and dozens of pamphlets under his belt. Orton, on the other hand, would have

---

8. *Public Ledger*, Philadelphia, Pennsylvania, January 12, 1856, 2.

9. This work, if it was ever published, does not appear to have survived.

10. Thomas M. McDade, "Lurid Literature of the Last Century: The Publications of E.E. Barclay," *Pennsylvania Magazine of History and Biography* 30 (October 1956): 454.

been an untested twenty-five year old making his first forays into the business of bad literature. All three pamphlets list the publishers as E.E. Barclay and A.R. Orton. And though all three were almost certainly printed in Philadelphia, their official places of publication moved from Louisville to Philadelphia to Detroit, depending on the story setting. One of these pamphlets lists no author on the title page, one lists "George Lippard" (who was a real mid-nineteenth-century author), and one lists "William Seldon" (the character whose journal purportedly comprises the pamphlet).[11] Finally, they each follow all of the writing formulas and conventions that Barclay had been using with great success for years.

From 1852 through 1855, Orton published at least fourteen more pamphlets under his own imprint—including *Boadicea; the Mormon Wife*.[12] Most of these list no author and have been attributed to Orton by subsequent catalogers. Because *Boadicea* does credit an editor on the title page, Alfreda Eva Bell has consistently been listed as the author—though most scholars consider it a pseudonym. The greatest objection to Orton's authorship is that Bell's second novel, *Rebel Cousins*, could not possibly have been written by Orton, as it was published nine years after Orton's death and treated events that he could not have foreseen.[13] The force of this objection diminishes substantially, however, when we consider that the publisher (and likely author) of *Rebel Cousins* was none other than E.E. Barclay, Orton's erstwhile collaborator—who certainly knew that Alfreda Eva Bell had been created to be part of one fiction and could there-fore be easily pressed into the service of another.

---

11. See the "Chronological List of Works Attributed to A.R. Orton" for the full titles and bibliographical information.

12. There could, of course, have been many more of these pamphlets that we do not know about. Given the low paper quality and unofficial distribution channels of these books, we are fortunate that any of them survived to be read today.

13. See, for example, Gordon, *The Mormon Question*, 251 note 56. Gordon assumes Bell's authorship of both an anti-Mormon novel (*Boadicea*) and an anti-slavery novel (*Rebel Cousins*) in a chapter of her book that discusses the connections between the anti-polygamy and the anti-slavery movements of the 1850s.

BOADICEA'S MORMONS

In the space of 82 pages, *Boadicea; the Mormon Wife* treats us to episodes of polygyny and polyandry, along with generous helpings of adultery, seduction, kidnapping, and no fewer than fourteen untimely, but spectacular deaths: people are shot, stabbed, bludgeoned, poisoned, hanged, strangled, and drowned. In the grand finale, four people are crushed by falling beams in a burning house. The body count places *Boadicea* even with the bloodiest of Shakespeare's tragedies, *Titus Andronicus*. And the Mormon society of *Boadicea* is so inherently unstable that we cannot imagine it lasting for more than a week or two after the novel closes. No other novel of the nineteenth century comes anywhere near *Boadicea* in portraying Mormon society as violent, chaotic, and dysfunctional.

When reading *Boadicea*, however, we must remember that, in 1855, most people knew very little about the seven-year-old Mormon settlement in the Great Basin. We should not expect anything like historical accuracy in a 15-cent pamphlet. But *Boadicea* does not even clear the relatively low bar set by books like *Female Lives Among the Mormons* and *Mormon Wives*. For one thing, the geography is impossibly cramped. Rather than inhabiting a sprawling desert empire, the Mormons of *Boadicea* all seem to inhabit a quaint, European-style mountain hamlet where everybody lives within easy strolling distance of the Great Salt Lake. The much-married leader of the Mormons—Bernard Yale, whose initials present him as a stand in for Brigham Young—is more like a corrupt small-town sheriff than the great leader and colonizer of American history.

Perhaps more significantly, though, the Mormon polygamy of the novel is not the rigid, patriarchal polygyny of history; it is more like the uninhibited polyamory of a 1970s rock festival. Men are free to marry other wives, even if those wives have other husbands. Though this standard is applied unevenly through the novel (many women are treated as virtual slaves by their husbands), it allows the author to introduce one of his most important villains of the novel: Cephysia Edmonds, the woman with whom Boadecia must share her beloved husband, Hubert. When Boadicea's husband Hubert brings Cephysia home to be his second wife—even after pledging lifelong faithfulness to Boadicea when they are married—the novel becomes a struggle between the two women for the soul of the man they share. Just as Boadicea is entirely good, Cephysia is pure evil. She tempts Hubert into polygamy, announces her intention to displace Boadicea, tries to poison her, and successfully murders Hubert Jr. with a strong dose of poison that she administers in plain sight of the boy's frantic mother.

The presence of such a villainous woman—who leaves one husband to marry another and then destroys the life of the man she supposedly loves—blunts somewhat the standard critique of polygamy as a system that gives men unfettered sexual license and reduces women to the status of slaves. But, *Boadicea; the Mormon Wife* is not really a political argument or a sophisticated moral allegory. It is a melodrama with a practically perfect heroine, moustache-twirling villains, larger-than-life perils, and people whose strange religion amplifies their menacing behaviors. And it was published the same year that A.R. Orton wrote and published similar treatments of Judaism (*The Life, Confession and Execution of The Jew and Jewess, Gustavus Linderhoff, and Fanny Victoria Talzingler*) and Islam (*The Turkish Spies Ali Abubeker Kaled and Zenobia Marrita Mustapha; Or, the Mohammedan Prophet of 1854*).

However, we can tell from the text that Orton did conduct some research on Mormonism before writing *Boadicea; the Mormon Wife*. The text reprints passages verbatim from at least two contemporary books: Henry Mayhew's nonfiction book *The Mormons, or, Latter-day Saints: A Contemporary History* (London, 1852), and Orvilla S. Belisle's novel *The Prophets; or, Mormonism Unveiled* (Philadelphia: Wm. White Smith, 1855). *The Prophets* was published the same year as *Boadicea*, and the address listed for its publisher is 195 Chestnut Street in Philadelphia—on the same block as the address given in 1855 for Orton's business, 116 Chestnut Street, making it likely that he would have encountered the book in the course of his regular business affairs. Both of these books would have been more helpful to someone researching Mormonism in Nauvoo and Missouri than in understanding the conditions of the Saints in Utah in 1855. In *The Mormons*, for example, Mayhew focuses his discussion of polygamy on the Nauvoo period, with its convoluted secrecy and its occasional polyandry. To create a depiction of Mormon society in Utah, Orton simply exported Mayhew's view of Nauvoo into a valley in the Rocky Mountains.

Though Orton does not seem to have taken any pains to create a historically accurate version of Mormon Utah, in at least one case, he ended up creating a prophetic one. In a side narrative describing the misfortunes of another woman in Utah, a French immigrant named Jeannette Boisrouge, Boadicea explains how her fiancé was killed by Mormons dressed as Indians:

> Her admirer and betrothed, Aldolphe Bertrand, a well-looking young French garçon, had been spirited mysteriously away. It was stated that the Indians had killed him, but one of the peccadilloes of the Mormons consists in disguising themselves in Indian costume, and waylaying such persons as are obnoxious to them, and putting them to death, after first appropriating such moneys as they might have about them. Numbers were known to have disappeared in this manner: the blame then fell upon the Indians, whom such of the colony as were deceived into believing them the true malefactors, became more than ever anxious to exterminate. Even those poor savages were incapable of committing deeds so infamous, so bloodthirsty, and so cruel, as were common practices of the Mormon Elders, under the name of religion. (81–82)

Had this passage been published two years later, after September 11, 1857, it would have blended in with thousands of fictional and ostensibly factual descriptions of the Mountain Meadows Massacre. However, in 1855, the image of Mormon Elders impersonating Indians and murdering settlers had not yet become a standard literary trope, though accusations of Mormons dressing up like Indians were not unknown in the popular press.

Boadicea; the Mormon Wife occupies a curious place in the history of both publishing and Mormonism because it does not fit comfortably in any of our standard categories. It is tempting to include *Boadicea* in the group of anti-Mormon novels with female narrators that appeared around the same time, but it doesn't really belong there. Its author was not a political activist or a crusading feminist—he was just a guy who figured out how to make a lot of money by presenting sensational crimes as true stories to an unsophisticated audience. Nor is it quite accurate to place *Boadicea* in the company of the dozens of dime novels about Mormon Utah published between 1860 and 1910. These novels were all working from a cultural script that involved Danites, blood atonement, and the Mountain Meadows Massacre—a script that Orton did not have access to because it had not yet been invented.

Boadicea; the Mormon Wife belongs to a sub-genre of crime fiction that flourished in the Eastern United States during the 1850s—a genre that was based on the "Newgate Calendar" criminal biographies of Great Britain. *Boadicea* has become increasingly important to scholars of Mormonism because it gives us a glimpse of the Mormon image in literature immediately after the Church's public acknowledgement of plural marriage. Over the next half century, this image would be sharpened and refined by writers with different rhetorical goals: to end polygamy, to attack Mormon theology, or just to tell a highly entertaining adventure story. In *Boadicea*, though, we see these tropes in their infancy, through a prolific author working at break-neck speed to imagine the lives of a strange people for readers willing to pay the "extremely low price of 15 cents" for the privilege of being amazed.

SOME NOTES ON THE TEXT AND APPENDICES

Boadicea; the Mormon Wife was originally published in 1855 by "Arthur R. Orton. Baltimore, Philadelphia, New York, and Buffalo." This has caused some scholars to look for evidence of authorship in Baltimore, the first-listed place of publication. However, given Orton's tendency to fictionalize publication places as well as authors, it is likely that the work was printed entirely in Philadelphia and then sold through Orton's network of travelling barkers in other cities. There is no information of how many copies were printed, but more than a dozen still exist in special collections (mainly in university libraries). For this many copies to have survived the ravages of time and poor-quality paper, there must have been a fairly large print run to begin with. Other pamphlets by Barclay and Orton boasted a circulation upwards of 10,000 copies, which is a reasonable estimate for *Boadicea* as well.

The text in this present edition has been transcribed as it was originally typeset, with original punctuation, spelling, and capitalization preserved. Original page numbers have been included in brackets {}. Illustrations have been reproduced from the original edition at the location in the text, though not necessarily in the same position on the page.

The two selections included in the appendices both come from sources that are reproduced, without acknowledgement, in the text of *Boadicea*. The first comes from Henry Mayhew's *The Mormons, or, Latter-day Saints: A Contemporary History* (1852), which Orton used to described Mormon worship services and hymnody. The selection excerpted here comes from Mayhew's chapter on Nauvoo polygamy, which Orton appears to have used as the basis for his understanding of polygamy in the Utah period, though he never cites nor quotes from it directly.

The second appendix is an extract from Orvilla S. Belisle's *The Prophets; or, Mormonism Unveiled*. This is a curious text to begin with. It is generally classified as a novel, but the fictional story is sandwiched between historical accounts of Mormonism. The first six chapters of the book detail the life of Joseph Smith and the development of Mormonism, with the story of Margaret Guilford—the patient wife who follows her deluded husband into Mormonism—comprising chapters 7 through 24. Chapter 25, from which we have drawn the excerpt in the appendix, returns to a non-fiction mode and gives an overview of Mormon Utah in 1855, one of the few such overviews available to Orton during the time that he was writing *Boadicea*.

A final note: the name "Boadicea" is an alternate spelling of "Boudica," who was the widow of a Celtic chieftain who led an uprising against the Roman forces in Britain in A.D. 60. Her name was properly pronounced *boo-duh-kuh*. Boadicea occurs infrequently as a girl's name in England and America and is usually pronounced *bow-duh-see-uh*, though instances of *bow-day-shuh* are not unknown. In December of 1853, the story "Sweet Bells Jangled" by George W. Curtis, featuring a heroine named Boadicea Fleurry, was published in *Harper's Magazine*.[14] The popularity of *Harper's*, combined with the rarity of the name Boadicea, make it likely that this was Orton's source for the name.

---

14. *Harper's New Monthly Magazine* 8 (December 1853–May 1854): 55–61.

A CHRONOLOGICAL LIST OF WORKS ATTRIBUTED TO A.R. ORTON

Year	Work	Author	Publication Information
1851	*The Bank Director's Son, a Real and Intensely Interesting Revelation of City Life. Containing an authentic account of the wonderful escape of the beautiful Kate Watson, from a flaming building in the city of Philadelphia.*	George Lippard	Philadelphia: E.E. Barclay and A.R. Orton, 1851.
1851	*The Avenger's Doom, or the Singular, Thrilling, and Exciting History and Lamentable Fate of J.O. Beauchamp and Miss Ann Cooke.*		Louisville, Ky.: E.E. Barclay and A.R. Orton, 1851.
1851	*The Extraordinary and All-Absorbing Journal of Wm. N. Seldon, One of a Party of Three Men Who Belonged to the Exploring Expedition of Sir John Franklin, and Who Left the Ship Terror, Frozen Up in Ice, in the Arctic Ocean, on the 10th. Day of June, 1850: Together with an Account of the Discovery of a New and Beautiful Country, Inhabited by a Strange Race of People.*	William N. Sheldon	Detroit, Mich.: E.E. Barclay and A.R. Orton, 1851.
1851	*The Arch fiend, or, The life, confession, and execution of Green H. Long . . . who was a member of that celebrated gang, known as the "Banditti of the West."*		New York: A.R. Orton, 1851.
1852	*The Life, career, and awful death by the garote [sic], of Margaret C. Waldegrave; otherwise, Margaret C. Florence—alias Mrs. Bellville, Madame Rolande, Madame Le Hocy, the poisoner and murderess, at Havanna, Cuba, June 9th, 1852. For the murder of Charles D. Ellas, Lorenzo Cordoval, and Pierre Dupont, (April 14th, 1852,) who were three desperate members of a powerful and sanguinary band of robbers, counterfeiters, and assassins, known as "the alumni."*		New Orleans, Charleston, Baltimore, Philadelphia: A.R. Orton, 1852.
1853	*"The Derienni"; or, Land pirates of the isthmus. Being a true and graphic history of robberies, assassinations, and other horrid deeds perpetrated by those cool-blooded miscreants, who have infested for years the great highway of California, the Eldorado of the Pacific . . . Together with the lives of three of the principal desperadoes as narrated by themselves.*		New Orleans, Charleston: A.R. Orton, 1853.

Year	Work	Author	Publication Information
1853	*Two eras in the life of the felon Grovenor I. Layton: who was lynched by the vigilance committee, at Sonora . . . California, June 17th, 1852: for robbery, murder, and arson . . .*		New Orleans, Charleston, Baltimore, Philadelphia: A.R. Orton, 1853.
1853	*The Eventful lives of Helen and Charlotte Lenoxa, the twin sisters of Philadelphia: with elaborate and minute details of the adventures, intrigues, and dark crimes, of these beautiful, but sinful women: the former of whom was hung . . . for the double murder of Captain Gerald Vernon, and his young wife ...*		Memphis, Richmond, Baltimore, Philadelphia: A.R. Orton, 1853.
1854	*The Autobiography of Charles Moore; revealing the history of the most remarkable robberies, forgeries, kidnapping, counterfeiting and gambling operations. And his terrible revenge in the murder of Richard White at Marseilles, France. : And a letter from Father Antoine, giving an account of his last words and death by the guillotine.*		Baltimore, Philadelphia, New York, Buffalo: A.R. Orton, 1854.
1854	*The Life of General M.D. Stanley, an American militia general: the celebrated roue, swindler, pickpocket, and murderer: who was executed at Vienna, Austria, September 17, 1853.*		Baltimore: A.R. Orton, 1854.
1855	*Hermann Remson, the great Louisiana murderer : the details of his first crime, his connection with the robbery of Davis, Palmer & Co.'s jewelry store, Boston, the murder of his accomplice at Buffalo and of Mrs. Campbell, Pike Co., Mississippi: also the atrocious murder of the venerable Judge Legree of Louisiana and his accomplished wife, and the burning of their beautiful mansion, consuming three children in the flames : with the strange & unnatural death, sunk in the quicksands of a lonely island in the Attakappas district of Louisiana.*	I.W. Spencer, A.R. Orton	Boston, Philadelphia, New York, Buffalo: A. R. Orton, 1855.
1855	*Isabella Narvaez: the female fiend and triple murderess, or, The life, confession and execution of Isabella Narvaez, the atrocious murderess of three husbands: who was hung at Shelbyville, Mo., Friday, Sept. 30, 1853.*	Isabella Narvaez; A.R. Orton	Baltimore: A.R. Orton, 1855.

Year	Work	Author	Publication Information
1855	*The three sisters, or, The life, confession, and execution of Amy, Elizabeth, and Cynthia Halzingler: who were tried, convicted, and executed, at Elizabethtown, Ark., Nov. 30, 1854, for the awful and horrible murder of the Edmonds family, consisting of seven members: together with the speech of the eldest sister, Amy, on the gallows*	O.R. Arthur, Rev., A.R. Orton, Frederick M. Coffin, John William Orr, George D. Wightman	Baltimore, Philadelphia, New York, Buffalo: A.R. Orton, 1855.
1855	*Boadicea; the Mormon Wife: Life-Scenes in Utah.*	Alfreda Eva Bell	Baltimore, Philadelphia, New York, Buffalo: Arthur R. Orton, [1855].
1855	*Love, Suicide, and Murder: The True History of the Unfortunate Loves of Mary Caroline Austin and Edgar Worthington; with the Full Particulars of Their Awful Suicide . . . the Trial of Worthington for that Crime, His Condemnation and Delivery from Prison by the People; His Escape . . . His Recapture, Dying Speech and Execution for Murder; His Wonderful Preservation from Death on the Gallows . . . and His Final Death*		Baltimore: Arthur R. Orton, 1855.
1855	*The Life, Confession and Execution of The Jew and Jewess, Gustavus Linderhoff, and Fanny Victoria Talzingler, who Were Hung in Ashville, North Carolina, Oct. 27, 1855, for The Triple Murder of Abner, Benjamin, and Charles Ecclangfeldt, Three Orphan Children Description: "The Making of the Modern Law: Trials, 1600–1926."*		Baltimore: A.R. Orton, 1855.
1855	*The Turkish Spies Ali Abubeker Kaled and Zenobia Marrita Mustapha; Or, the Mohammedan Prophet of 1854. A True History of the Russo-Turkish War. By Lieutenant Murray of the Allied Armies now in Turkey.*	Maturin Murray Ballou	Baltimore, Philadelphia, New York, Buffalo: A.R. Orton, 1855.

BOADICEA;

THE MORMON WIFE

LIFE-SCENES IN UTAH

edited by

Alfreda Eva Bell

1855

LAND OF THE HONEY-BEE.

CHAPTER I.

THE "LAND OF THE HONEY-BEE."

The Young Couple—Their Appearance—Description of a Mormon Ceremony—Mormon Hymns—Conversation of Hubert and Boadicea—Professions of Hubert.

{15} There is a lovely valley situated midway between the States of the great Mississippi and the shores of the Pacific Ocean. To this terrestrial paradise, its present inhabitants, the Mormons, have given the name of Deseret (De-ser-ét), a word of mystic import, signifying "The Land of the Honey-Bee."

The Mormons have settled in the depression styled the "Great Basin," a region bounded by the Rocky Mountain land, out of which no waters flow.

In one of the open lots where the Mormons were in the habit of worshiping, somewhat apart from the crowd, and side by side, stood a young couple observing a religious ceremony.

This couple, a man about twenty-two, and a girl of seventeen years of age, were remarkable for personal beauty. The girl's countenance was striking, noble in expression and feature; her eyes were blue, dark, and clear, receiving a peculiar softness from being nearly half {16} concealed in long eyelashes of a golden brown; they sparkled as a narrow line of water will glitter between borders of long reeds, when glancing in the summer sun. The young girl's tresses were soft, fine, and glossy, filled with abrupt spots of light and deep shadows, caused by the rich waves with which their luxuriance was broken, and were gathered carelessly into a knot, classical and beautiful, because natural and untortured by art. The form of the maiden was perfect, of medium height, suggesting strength, while naught but softness and beauty appeared in its delicate and rounded outlines.

She stood as if scarce resting on the ground, with such lightness did her form seem posed. Her countenance wore an expression of mingled perplexity and interest.

The young man was tall, graceful in carriage. His features were regular, his expression intellectual; the most remarkable feature in his face being a pair of large black eyes, the burning brilliancy of which he appeared to be making a constant effort to subdue. The character of his mouth was at times repulsive, but generally wore an expression of sweetness and reflection.

The maiden's attention was wholly given to the passing ceremony. The youth's eyes were fixed on her alone. A senior priest (*Saint,* Elder, or Brother, as they are called,) was asking a blessing on the congregation as they stood in the open air; the exercises of religion (!) followed. The accents of the following hymn then filled the air. It was sung harmoniously, but with that mad, fanatical enthusiasm, which shows the power of the Evil One to take possession of mind and body, and pervert God's gift, the immortal soul, to insane wickedness under the name of religion. Religion! the French proverb—

"Derriere la croix, se carbe souvent le diable," or,

"Behind the cross, the devil is often hid," was never more applicable than of the *Mormon faith.*

A MORMON HYMN.[1]

> Ye chosen twelve, to ye are given
> The keys of this last ministry;

---

1. Bell's "First Mormon Hymn" originally appeared as part of Parley P. Pratt's, "Mission of the Twelve," which was first published in *The Millennium, a Poem, to which Is Added Hymns and Songs on Various Subjects New and Interesting, Adapted to the Dispensation of the Fullness of Times*

To every nation under Heaven,
From land to land, from sea to sea.

First to the Gentiles sound the news,
Throughout Columbia's happy land;
And then before it reach the Jews,
Prepare on Europe's shores to stand.

Let Europe's towns and cities hear
The Gospel tidings; angels bring
The Gentile nations far and near—
Prepare their hearts His praise to sing. {17}

Listen, ye islands of the sea,
For every isle shall hear the sound;
Nations and tongues before unknown,
Though long since lost, shall soon be found!

And then again shall Asia hear,
Where angels first the news proclaimed;
Eternity shall record bear,
And earth repeat the loud Amen.

The nations catch the pleasing sound,
And Jew and Gentile swell the strain;
Hosannah o'er the earth resound;
Messiah soon shall come to reign!

Here followed another prayer, made extempore, and then another song, so characteristic of the Mormons that we give it here. It was sung to the tune, "The Rose that all are Pra+ising;"—all sorts of music, profane, even *comic*, as well as sacred, being used in Mormon *worship*.

SECOND MORMON HYMN.[2]

The God that others worship, is not the God for me!
He has no parts or body, and cannot hear or see!

(Boston, 1835), 49–50. It appeared in several early editions of the LDS Hymnal, including the 1849 Liverpool Edition, where it found its way as an example of Mormon hymnody in Henry Mayhew's book, *The Mormons, or, Latter-day Saints: A Contemporary History* (London, 1852, 37–38). As much of this chapter is taken verbatim from Mayhew's book, it must be considered Orton's most likely source for information on the Mormons.

2. "The God that Others Worship, Is Not the God for Me!" first appeared in the New York LDS newspaper, *The Prophet*, on June 29, 1944, attributed

But I've a God that lives above,
  A God of power and of love,
A God of Revelation,—Oh, that's the God for me!
Oh, that's the God for me! Oh, that's the God for me!

A church without apostles, is not the church for me!
It's like a ship dismasted, afloat upon the sea!
  But I've a church that's always led,
  By the twelve stars around its head—
A church with good foundations,—Oh, that's the church for me!
Oh, that's the church for me! Oh, that's the church for me!

A church without a prophet, is not the church for me!
It has no head to lead it: in it I would not be!
  But I've a church not built by man,
  Cut from the mountain without hands—
A church with gifts and blessings,—Oh, that's the church for me!
Oh, that's the church for me! Oh, that's the church for me!

The hope the Gentiles cherish, is not the hope for me!
It has no hope for knowledge—far from it I would be!
  But I've a hope that will not fail,
  That reaches safe within the vail—
Which hope is like an anchor,—Oh, that's the hope for me!
Oh, that's the hope for me! Oh, that's the hope for me!

The heaven of sectarians, is not the heaven for me!
So doubtful its location, neither on land nor sea!
  But I've a heaven on the earth, (!)
  The land and home that gave me birth—
A heaven of light and knowledge,—Oh, that's the heaven for me!
Oh, that's the heaven for me! Oh! that's the heaven for me!

Then followed a sermon from some one previously appointed
to preach, setting forward the merits and righteousness of having
a number of wives; stating that in so doing consisted "taking up
the burden of the cross!" and that all women must be damned who

_____

to John Hardy. It was later reprinted, unattributed, in *Times and Seasons* 6,
no. 2 (February 1845): 799, with instructions that it be sung to the tune
of the Irish song, "The Rose that All Are Praising." Mayhew cited the latter
source when he reprinted it in *The Mormons* (39–40). The song was included
in several mid-nineteenth-century Mormon hymnbooks, including the 1951
Liverpool edition. See Michael Hicks, *Mormonism and Music: A History*
(Champaign, Ill.: University of Illinois Press, 2003), 66–67.

HUBERT AND BOADICEA CONVERSING ON THE MORMON DOCTRINE.

were not married; that it would be impossible for any virgin to enter heaven, on the principle that it was necessary for every woman
to have a man—a husband to take her into heaven. {18}

{19} Were this belief current among us, (the *Gentiles*, as the
Mormons call us,) I am afraid that there is no hope for divers and
sundry ladies of my acquaintance, if they cannot go to heaven till
their husbands go!!!!

The service was continued by exhortations and remarks from
several *Saints*, who were "moved to speak," and that upon an extraordinary variety of subjects, such as are not commonly supposed
fitting to be introduced into religious worship. Many secular matters being arranged, the congregation ("of vipers") was dismissed
with a blessing.

The young couple, who had stood during the greater part of this
ceremony, now walked away. The countenance of the girl was pale
and deeply anxious. The expression of the youth's face seemed to ask
her thoughts. At last the maiden, to whom we shall give the name
of Boadicea, spoke.

"This country is a second Garden of Eden; yet, Hubert, the
thought that it is profaned by a community of wives and husbands,
is to me loathsome, frightful! In spite of all that surrounds me,
something innate with me revolts against this state of things."

The girl spoke with deep and pure enthusiasm and earnestness.
"I feel," continued she, "that heaven has rightly ordained, that one
woman shall belong to one man, to one man alone, if possible, for the
term of their two lives, and that they shall keep themselves apart from
all others, each sanctified to the other for each other's sake. In such a
union *alone* can perfect love, harmony, and happiness exist. Purity in
thought, in deed, in life, is *impossible*, I believe, without it. Tell me,
Hubert! does it not make *you* happy, to think that *I* think thus, that
I thus believe; does it make you happy to feel that you suffice for the
perfect happiness of *one* human being, loving and constant, who asks
nothing in this life but the continuance of *your* love?"

"Ah! Boadicea!" answered Hubert, "you speak from the impulse
of a naturally pure mind.; Pure yourself, you are not tempted to
swerve from the path of honorable devotion to one, and to one
alone. I too have but one earthly wish, that we should remain con-

BOADICEA RETURNING TO HER DWELLING.

stant to each other: I wold willingly hold myself aloof from all others for your sake."

He spoke with sincerity. Hubert at that time sincerely loved Boadicea. Theirs, indeed, were hearts so formed for each other, so fitted for becoming perfected, through the holy influence of a single and constant love, that but for the fatal fatuity which surrounded them—the facilities, the temptations to error—they would have presented to the world the miracle of constancy, of true and perfect love.

The errors of the man would have ceased through the influence of the woman, and the softness of her nature been elevated into a higher intellectual grade, by the influence of the superior mind and native grandeur of the man. But, alas! they lived in a hell. Their present faith, their present constancy and love, were little short of a miracle, with such vicious and diabolic surroundings.

{20} "And do you willingly promise me never to swerve, then, unless *I* change, dear Hubert?" said Boadicea.

"I promise it with all my heart," answered Hubert; "nay, more, if *I* ever depart from the promises I now utter, of faithful adherence to you, I will even exile myself from hope, and condemn myself to wretchedness and punishment forever, by swearing never to approach you more; never again to ask you to listen to words like these."

"I believe you," answered Boadicea, with a deep emotion of gratitude to heaven for such love on earth. And, indeed, at that moment, Hubert *believed himself.*

They parted—the heart, the soul of the girl filled with a perfect trust in the young man—such trust as a child feels in its parents. There is nothing more confiding than a woman's heart, when she loves,—no confidence more blind;—after experience ever teaches that such faith belongs to God *alone.*

MORMON MARRIAGE.

CHAPTER II.

The Marriage of Boadicea and Hubert—The Mormon Articles of Faith—
One of the Characteristics of the Mormon Belief—Remarks on the
Mormons.

{21} Within a few weeks after this conversation, the marriage of
boadicea and Hubert took place. Each was under the influence of
the wild, blind faith in happiness, and in each other, which is the
fanaticism, as well as the religion, of love.

All arrangements for the ceremony were made by the young
people themselves, the parents of each being too much engrossed in
religion, to be diverted therefrom by so trifling and unimportant a
matter as the marriage of a son or daughter.

The mother of Boadicea, a beautiful woman, merely smiled
scornfully at the expressions of affection for Hubert which fell from
her daughter's lips, and replied that "she had no doubt they would be
content with each other *for awhile;* people generally were," she said;
"but soon changed in heir feelings; which proved the merit of the
Mormon faith, since it permitted them to follow the dictates of their
own involuntary feelings, by changing when and as often as they
pleased, without either party being therefore excluded from society."

"*Society!* the society of the Mormon settlements consists of black-legs, murderers, forgers, swindlers, gamblers, thieves, and adulterers! *Select*, certainly! {22}

We take this occasion to reveal the creed, the articles of Faith, of the "Latter Day Saints."

CREED OF THE MORMONS.[1]

(This creed is taken from the Mormon religious works, *ad verbatim*, and is given without alteration or addition of any kind.)

"We believe in God, the Eternal Father, and his Son, Jesus Christ, and in the Holy Ghost.

"We believe that men will be punished for their own sins, and not for Adam's transgressions.

"We believe that, through the atonement of Christ, all mankind may be saved, by obedience to the laws and ordinances of the gospel.

"We believe these ordinances are: 1st, Faith in the Lord Jesus Christ; 2d, Repentance; 3d, Baptism by immersion, for the remission of sins; 4th, Laying on of Hands for the Gift of the Holy Spirit; 5th, the Lord's Supper.

"We believe that men must be called of God by inspiration, and by laying on of hands from those who are d exactly uly commissioned to preach the Gospel, and administer the ordinances thereof.

"We believe in the same organization that existed in the primitive Church, viz.: Apostles, Prophets, pastors, teachers, Evangelists, etc.

"We believe in the powers and gifts of the everlasting Gospel, viz.: The Gift of Faith! *The discerning of spirits! Prophecy! Revelation! Visions! Healing! Tongues! and the Interpretation of Tongues!* Wisdom! Charity! Brotherly Love, etc.

"We believe in the Word of God, recorded in the Bible; *we also believe in the Word of God, recorded in the Book of Mormon; and in all other good books!!!*

"We believe all that God has revealed, all that he does now reveal; *and we believe that He will reveal many more great and important things, pertaining to the kingdom of God, and Messiah's second coming!!!*

---

1. The "Creed of the Mormons," which consists of a variant of the Thirteen Articles of Faith now published in the LDS Pearl of Great Price, appears much as it appears in Mayhew's *The Mormons*, 40–41. Bell, however, has added a fair number of exclamation points and italicization for emphasis.

[NO CAPTION]

"We believe in the literal gathering of Israel, and the restoration of the ten tribes; that Zion will be established on the western continent; that Christ will reign personally upon the earth a thousand years, and that the earth will be renewed, and receive its paradisiacal glory.

"We believe in the literal resurrection of the body, and that the rest of the dead live not again until the thousand years are expired.

"We claim the privilege of worshiping the Almighty *according to the dictates of our conscience*, (!) unmolested, and allow men the same privilege—let them worship when or where they may.

"We believe in being subject to Kings, Queens, Presidents, Rulers, and magistrates; in obeying, honoring and sustaining the law!

"We believe in being *honest!* true! CHASTE!! temperate! bene-{23} volent! virtuous!!!! and upright!!!!! and in doing good to all men; indeed we may say, that we follow the admonition of Paul: we *'believe all things!'* we *'hope all things!!'* we have endured very many things, and hope to be able to *endure all things!!!!!* Every thing love, *virtuous*, praiseworthy, and *of good report*, we seek after, looking forward to the recompense of reward! But an idle or lazy person cannot be a Christian—neither have salvation. He is a drone, and destined to be *stung to death*, and tumbled out of the hive."

Perhaps, if asked, the Mormons would account for the permanent and mysterious disappearance of numerous individuals, who have revolted against their horrors, and threatened to leave them, by saying that they were *"stung to death and tumbled out of the hive."* Numerous and surprising as these mysterious disappearances have been, no inquiry is ever instituted among the Mormons for missing persons.

These articles of faith have the remarkable merit of being alterable to suit all occasions and emergencies, which is, indeed, the chief characteristic of the Mormon religion. Their *spiritual* doctrine is "of the earth, earthy." It must, we hope, sooner or later, destroy itself, like a hideous monster feeding on its own body. Its very nature is such that it must be self-consumed;—the sooner the better.

Boadicea and Hubert married. We now present Boadicea as her own historian. Herself shall relate her own painful revelation of unutterable misery.[2]

---

2. At this point, *Boadicea; the Mormon Wife* shifts to a first-person narrative told through the narrative device of Boadicea's own diary.

CEPHYSIA.

CHAPTER III.

JOURNAL OF BOADICEA.—PART I.

The Coming Home—Misgivings—Forebodings—Arrangements—Fear of
Misunderstanding—Boadicea's Reserve— Trust—Description of Two
Pictures—Visit of Two Mormon Women—Insulting Nature of their
Remarks—Demand of Cephysia—Refusal of Boadicea—Conduct of
Hubert—Departure of the women—Illness of Boadicea.

{24} That was a lovely day, on which Hubert and I went home.
Home! how strangely the word sounded—how sweet its whispered
promise of seclusion!—for among the Mormons, the peculiar sanc-
tity of home is unknown. There is not that privacy, that secluded
retreat, which makes every house, where things are as they should
be, a sort of Penetralia, or Inner temple, a *Sanctum Sanctorum*.

Hubert was in glorious spirits. He insisted upon draping the
looking-glass with my bridal vail, and kept continually arranging

my long hair in different forms; then suddenly carried me in his arms to the glass, "to see how like an angel on a cloud" I looked.

The vail fell around the brilliant surface of the mirror in mist-like folds, and I did not observe at first, that the frame Hubert had con- {25} cealed therewith was black. When I noticed this, a peculiar shudder thrilled my frame, and Hubert, on whose arm I was leaning, asked me if I felt cold. I answered, "No," and smiled at my own folly, as I thought it then.

Yet my eyes would rivet themselves, a thousand times a day, on the frame of the mirror, until I began to fancy, at last, that it looked like the outline of a little coffin. Then I roused myself again, and said in my heart, "What have I to do with sad thoughts, I, who am so much beloved?"

In my own strength of spirit I defied Fate. Alas! alas! the heart of a woman is too often willfully blind to what *may be* faint whispers from a spirit-land.

I have ever thought that the beautiful should surround us in everyday life, lest, amid the commonplace, we should forget the very existence of the poetry of life; beautiful objects, sweet sounds, works of art and literature, to remind us of the great souls which have been, and may be again; and it was, therefore, that I soon managed to arrange a room purposely for our sitting-room, where Hubert and I could spend a great portion of our time—our leisure hours, surrounded by the poetical atmosphere which the beautiful creates.

Hubert insisted on having placed among my treasures a bust of Joseph Smith, the Mormon prophet. I did not wish this, for to me that countenance is repellant, as it is coarse, cunning, and full of low passions, sensuality, and every mean and cowardly vice.

It remained where Hubert placed it, however, for I soon found that, while seeming to consult *my* wishes, he usually obtained his own will. I would not say much about the disagreeable-looking bust, because I had a horrible dread of *the first quarrel.* There was something in the expression of Hubert's eyes which was at times fierce and vindictive, and the *first quarrel* assumed the shape of the sword of Damocles, and seemed to hang over me suspended by a mere thread, which I could imagine was swayed to and fro, and quivered at Hubert's least impatient word, or slightest frown.

This made me constrained and awkward sometimes, and then Hubert would fix his large black eyes upon me with an impatient expression, very piercing and unpleasant, which only increased my trouble. If he looked in the least "savage," as he himself would call it, in his merrier moods, it caused me to have an actual palpitation of the heart.

Men should remember that a delicate woman conceals half her affection, as well as half of all her emotions, and that nature teaches us to appear often cold and constrained when we are most troubled at heart, lest we have offended the one beloved object. How often is this very delicacy of manner, arising from delicacy of mind, turned against us—how often do men say of the legal object of their love, "She is a very cold sort of woman," and this in excuse for wanderings from the path of right! Ah! it is because all women feel instinctively that the strongest-minded men may, like children, be {26} surfeited with sweets. It is only a woman who really cares very little to preserve the *constant* love of one man, that will give her whole self, without reserve, heart and soul at once.

Women should never forget that marriage is a holy and *"honorable"* state, and that while fulfilling all its duties, they will only endear themselves the more to *a pure and noble mind*, by being in outward manner as pure as vailed vestals.

Yet how often are men of fine mind misled into mistaking, for true affection, utter unreserve! No, no! That woman who does not sincerely wish to preserve a certain involuntary feeling of deep respect, even in the most intimate relations of marriage, would soon change, soon vary, for she herself tears away the flimsy vail which should always drape the statue; and with satiety comes changefulness, as well to herself as to her husband.

I thought I did right with regard to Hubert. The future proved that in a happier, purer state of society, my creed was the right one, and would have been triumphant as the true one, for, in spite of all, Hubert loved, *now loves me,* with a pure love, which even the temptations he yielded to could not utterly destroy while he still lived on earth. Others have taken from me the man himself, but I shall always believe, nay, now I *know* that I shall always reign the *immortal queen of his soul. In heaven Hubert will be mine again.*

The furniture of our boudoir consisted of the usual articles—pictures, statues, books, etc. I had chosen old and choice ones, that they might possess for the longest possible time the charm of novelty.

Over the mantlepiece hung a curious picture by a German artist, who possessed that singular turn of mind, so common to his countrymen, which led him to blend the terrible, the hideous, the grotesque—in a word, "the horrible," with every thing beautiful which his pencil created.[1]

This picture represented a chasm between two rocks—neither the summit nor the base was visible—but the cleft conveyed a terrible impression of isolation and unfathomable depth. I presume the artist thought of the *"bottomless pit."*

Midway between the top and bottom of the picture, and seeming suspended in the air, was the figure of a man of graceful frame—whose form was thrown backward in an attitude of the most abject despair. As he seemed suspended, the shoulders and waist were most distinct in the fearful dimness which constituted the atmosphere of the picture.

Far above the form of the man, and smiling down upon him, appeared an angelic female face—pale, tearful, yet with a saintly smile of hope. It seemed the face of Purity herself—holy, yet human.

Far below the man, and wearing an expression of malignant rage, scowled another female face. The features of this face were symmetrical—even beautiful—but indicative of coarse, ungoverned pas- {27} sions, made more fiendish by the look of envious anger it wore. It was the very beauty of Evil, even as the face of the fair woman seemed the beauty of Holiness and of Good.

In gazing upon the picture, a faint light, which seemed shed from the eyes of the fairer face, appeared to fall upon the brow of

---

1. The drawings described here have some features in common with the works of such German painters as Jakob Wilhelm Mechau (1745–1808) and Caspar David Friedrich (1774–1840). The latter's most famous painting, "Wanderer above the Sea of Fog" (1818) contains just the sort of "chasm between two rocks" described. It is conceivable that Bell could have encountered such paintings and drawings, though it is unlikely that any young married couples in Salt Lake City in 1855 had the resources to decorate their homes with German Romantic art. The two paintings described symbolically foreshadow the events of the novel.

the man, to brighten it and that despairing face to glow with a faint glimmer of something resembling hope.

The companion picture to this one represented the same man raised from the chasm into the light of a glorious sky. His arms encircled the neck of the fair woman, whose cheek rested against his own. The twain seemed to soar in purest ether.

Far, far below, in the very depths of the yawning and cloven rock, was the fearful face, with shining, glittering eyes, of the dark woman. It looked upward with an expression of the most furious and deadly hate. A serpent, looking instinct with life, entwined her throat. . . . . . .

One of the statues which I had grouped about our room represented Ondine crouched beneath a little fountain of water—the water being skillfully represented by glass. She awaited the approach of her lover, who, in his hunting-dress, knelt on the brink of the fountain—his ear bent to the waves. A water-lily, exquisitely chiseled in the marble, rippled the surface of the glassy fount.[2]

On the opposite side knelt a tiny marble Cupid, under the shadow of a large leaf, fashioned to support bouquets of flowers.

In a basket of moss, near the boy Cupid, was piled a heap of fruit of wax—grapes, apples, oranges, pines, nectarines and cherries—my own handiwork. Among the fruit I had placed autumn leaves and the many-colored grasses, which seem as if they were the little trees of Fairy Land. . . . . . .

I had not long been installed in my new home before a change took place in Hubert's manner. Painful, unaccountable indifference took the place of his former kindness, passionate tenderness and warm affection. His absences from home were long and of frequent occurrence. After them he seemed invariably gloomy, moody, and averse to conversation. I gradually relapsed into the same cold and

---

2. Ondine in French folklore is a water nymph who sacrificed her immortality in order to marry a human. Her human husband promises to be faithful to her, but he is not. When she discovers him with another woman, she curses him never to sleep again. Throughout the nineteenth century, the story of Ondine (German: Undine) was incorporated into novels, plays, and operas. Like the drawings described earlier in this chapter, the story of Ondine foreshadows Hubert's impending infidelity to Boadicea.

reserved manner. It became a habit with me to conceal my affection for Hubert.

Natural feelings of pride will induce every woman to pursue the same course, if she believe that the fault is not in herself, and have deep faith in a return of merited affection.

I never questioned Hubert with regard to his frequent and long absences from home. I acted as if I had not missed him. I welcomed him invariably as if he had been a dear brother, nothing more.

At first he seemed surprised; then he grew angry; at last *he* reproached *me* with fickleness. Oh, man! man!

I said not one word, but a moment after he had left me in anger, he might, had he returned, have found me weeping such desolate, bitter, burning tears, as women shed only when their holiest affections, {28} their deepest feelings are outraged, and they are made to feel a sort of shame at what is rarest and best among their heart's emotions. . .

One day Hubert returned from one of his long absences, accompanied by two women on horseback. One, a tall brunette, immediately appeared to me to bear a strong resemblance to the dark woman in my German pictures, and this, in spite of handsome features, abundant black hair, and a form which, though too full for beauty, was not without a certain degree of symmetry. A horrible shudder passed over my frame as this woman entered the sitting-room. I felt a fearful presentiment that my destiny was linked with hers, for what horrors I knew not; but the hand of death itself seemed to gripe [sic] my heart.

The name of this woman was Cephysia Edmonds. I have been told that her family in the States, or among the Gentiles, as the Mormons would say, was respectable and of good standing, but that her conduct had been so shameless, since her assumption of the Mormon doctrines, that they held no communication with her, and even disowned her as their daughter.

She informed me that she was one of Elder Manor's wives, and manifested an extraordinary interest in my domestic affairs, every now and then glancing at Hubert in a manner that left no doubt in my mind as to her being his mistress.

Greatly to my astonishment, the brunette informed me that she was commissioned to ask me if I felt willing to become the spiritual wife of Elder Aaron Manor, her husband, who, she informed, had only ten wives already, and wished to add myself to his already "*small* and *respectable*" family. With the utmost indignation, I told her that I loved my husband, and that Hubert and I, though unable to leave the Mormon settlement, were only *in*, not *of* it, and were determined to leave it as soon as we could, and never to conform to the Mormon doctrines, either outwardly or in our domestic arrangements.

Cephysia Edmonds hereupon burst into a loud laugh, at the same time winking in the most indelicate manner at Hubert, who, to my surprise, joined in the laugh, and desired her to "let Boadicea alone."

She then informed me that this was what many had said *at first;* that her first husband, Myers Brown, had said the same thing exactly, but that he had three other wives beside herself now, and that she had been the "spiritual wife" of two other husbands![3]

Her companion, a slender woman with yellow hair, and rather pretty, joined in the laughter, though in hollow tones, which were those of laughter without mirth, and replied that "all the men said so at first," and that all first wives talked the same way that I was talking, but they soon "changed their tune," she said.

The brown woman now took it into her head to fancy the basket of wax fruit, and asked me to "make her a present of it." I declined, upon the ground that it formed part of the furniture of the room, when Hubert, to my utter consternation, frowning at me, {29} and muttering something about "rudeness," detached the little corbeille from its ivory pedestal, and handed it to Cephysia, who thereupon made me a mocking courtesy, and gravely thanked me "for nothing."

I did not utter one word, though I felt myself turn pale with astonishment, as much as with grief. I had spent such pleasant hours by Hubert's side, moulding the delicate waxen fruit, arranging the pretty leaves, and he had so much admired the little toy.

I quitted the room—the sharp triumphant laughter of Cephysia rang in my ears as I closed the door. I heard her say something witty,

---

3. In the world of *Boadicea*, women are no more bound by the principles of monogamy than men are; women who are already married to men can be married to other men, who are also married to other women (some of whom are married to other men). The Mormonism that she imagines, then, is one of unrestrained sexual license for both genders.

HUBERT WITH THE MORMON WOMEN LEAVES BOADICEA.

of course, about "all the wives" being "*touchy*" at first, and she also applauded Hubert's conduct, advising him, at the same time, to "keep the upper hand."

About five minutes after, the women rode away, as they had come, accompanied by *Hubert—my husband*—mine, alas! no more.

As the hoofs of the horses disappeared, I fell on the floor in a deep swoon.

The happiness of the few short months previous to this occurrence, were all the calm, peaceful happiness I have ever known, except the feeling resembling satisfaction with which I reflect, that, in spite of all which afterwards occurred, I am still a pure wife.

CHAPTER IV.

JOURNAL OF BOADICEA.—PART II.

Return of Hubert—Forgiveness—Mormon Polygamy.

{30} I WILL not attempt to depict the feelings with which I saw Hubert return after the lapse of two days. My health, at that time delicate—I was, indeed, about to become a mother—suffered severely from what I had been called upon to bear. Such was the secret grief which I endured that I almost feared that the child I was about to bring into the world would be an idiot.

Hubert offered no apology. His return afforded no relief, for it had now become painful to me to see him. I would willingly have fled from the very sound of that voice, so altered from its affectionate tones to those of harshness and even of brutal insult. And yet, after a time, he again caressed me, as if nothing had happened; and I—my heart benumbed, as it were, with grief—suffered his now unwelcome caresses in patient silence—while ever between us seemed to rise the mocking phantom of the dark woman, in an attitude of derision. I felt that Hubert's professions of renewed love and promises of amendment were hollow. My peace of mind—my respect for and confidence in him, were fled forever.

Oh! in the social (*very* social) system of the Mormons, a wife may be subjected to the grossest insult one moment and *obligingly* caressed the next. Her husband may—such is the caprice and so coarse the passions of some men—greet her with apparent affection, while the kisses of some one of the courtesan wives of another man re still warm upon his lips.

The wife is not expected to show the slightest emotion, even if sure of this, and may esteem herself fortunate if not duly delivered over to another man, upon the strength of some "revelation," made to the husband *at his own request*, through the intervention of the Elders. She is generally apprised that her eternal welfare depends upon her becoming "sealed to"—which means the wife of—no! the *mistress* of some other member of the Mormon community.

According to the Mormon creed—I repeat—no woman can enter heaven on her own merits—that is, *without a man to take her there! ! ! ! ! !* This convenient and highly moral arrangement causes not only a community of *wives* and *husbands*, but also a community of *mothers* and *fathers;* so that, after a time—if the Mormon settlement be not broken up and destroyed by dispersion—it will be as great a proof of wisdom for a mother to know who is the father of her own child, as it will be for that child to know who really are his own parents.

BOADICEA VISITING MARGARET.

CHAPTER V.

JOURNAL OF BOADICEA.—PART III.

Desertion and Death of a Mormon Woman.

{31} I was passing, one morning, near a small house, and was attracted by hearing low moans from within. Not having acquired the callousness to suffering, which is a characteristic of the *benevolent* Mormon association, I entered, without hesitation, the room whence these sounds appeared to proceed.

On a pile of clothes, arranged so as to serve as a bed, and emaciated to the last degree, lay a woman groaning with pain. She was alone, and scarcely noticed my entrance. Seeing that it was necessary to obtain help, I sought all over the building for some one to assist me. In the adjoining room to the sufferer were several other wives of the same husband, Elder Thomas Lincoln; and upon my {32} demanding assistance, one of them said, "Pretty face, take yourself off—whoever you are, don't be showing yourself here. Margaret is in labor pains. She'll never live through it. She's a poor, miserable, puling, ailing thing, not worth minding. Just let her be; she'll go off easy after it's all over."

"Yes," said another; "she is of no use to any one since she lost her health. Elder Abel White says, that it is not 'a good act' to assist her, for she talks against us Mormons. I hope she'll die, and the brat too."

"Yes," said another, named Hannah—a pretty woman; "she had better be left to reflect. The sooner she is *free* the better."

"Are you women," I answered, "and do you answer me thus?"

"Women! to be sure we are. We wish we were not, though."

"Will you not assist me?" reiterated I, hearing the cries of the woman Margaret.

"No!" answered one and all.

I left the inhuman wretches and sought the chamber of Margaret, who in a few hours brought into the world a dead and deformed child, and expired in agony, after blessing me and entreating me to have her decently laid out and interred.

> "Can such things be,
> And overcome us like a summer cloud,
> Without our special wonder!"[1]

I felt harrowed to the inmost heart at her wild, despairing words. Among the Mormons it is held "unnecessary" to endure the sight of suffering. When any one falls sick, the Elders are consulted as to whether it is better to aid and assist them or not. If the party or parties be obnoxious to any one, they are left to die upon the strength of some "vision" or "revelation."

The illnesses of frequent occurrence among the Mormons are of the most startling and surprising nature. I have seen several deaths which I could have solemnly testified were by poison. Of these no notice was taken, it being asserted that, to attempt to assist these persons, would have been "presuming to attempt to alter the decrees" of Providence.

Sometimes it is said that no assistance must be rendered, lest it "prolong a life of sin." This is in cases of revolt from Mormonism, this being the only sin really furnished among this *virtuous* and *enlightened* people.

---

1. From Shakespeare's *MacBeth*, Act III, scene 4, lines 109–11.

BROTHER SETH AT HIS PRIVATE DEVOTIONS.

CHAPTER VI.

JOURNAL OF BOADICEA.—PART IV.

Visit of Brother Seth Holmes—His Attempt to induce Boadicea to become his "Spiritual" Wife—Answer of Boadicea–Insulting Conduct of Brother Seth—Cowardice of Seth.

{33} ONE morning, during one of Hubert's now frequent absences, a man—dressed like a gentleman—but, as the sequel will show, without other pretensions to that title, entered my house without knocking or asking admittance. Without preamble he seated himself opposite me and began to speak.

"Sister Boadicea," said he, "I wish to ask you a few questions. Will you answer them?"

"Yes, sir," said I.

"To speak plainly," continued Brother Seth Holmes—for this was the man's name—"have you not an affection for me,—such—

that, were it lawful and right, you would accept me for your husband and companion?"

"I never saw you before in my life," answered I.

"Why, yes, you have, beloved Sister Boadicea," answered the man—"at worship."

I stared at him. "Well," answered I, at last, "I do remember seeing your ugly phiz before." {34}

"Be serious, sister, be serious," answered the *pious* Elder. "Brother Peter Smith has had a revelation from God that it is lawful and right for me to have you for a wife."

I started back and stared at the man.

"Brother Smith has seven wives himself, and I have nine; but I would rather have you for a wife than any of them—or the nine together—if you will be my spiritual wife and be 'sealed unto' me next week. I will even dismiss all the others—which is not generally done, I assure you, and get them new husbands. For, as it was in the days of Abraham, so it shall be in these last days; and whoever is among the first that is willing to take up the cross, will receive the greatest of all earthly blessings possible. And if you will accept me, I will take you straight to the celestial kingdom. And if you will have me in this world, I will have you in the next world. And Brother Peter will marry us next week. And you can hold your tongue until I clear my house out for you, and your husband will not know any thing about it. It's none of his business. You know he is in love with Cephysia, Elder Aaron Manor's wife. He'll not mind it in the least, I assure you." (!)

"Have you done?" answered I; "because if you have, you had better go. My husband will be here directly; and I will tell him exactly what you say; and he will thrash you within an inch of your life."

"Look here, Sister Boadicea; don't you believe in me? You'd better believe in me. What I tell you is lawful and right, before God—according to holy revelation. You have the foolish notions of the Gentiles of the States; but I can tell you you had better behave yourself, and do as I reveal to you, or we shall have to get rid of you in some quiet way or other, for rebelling against the institutions of the holy faith, lest you should breed discord here, after the manner of the blind and unrighteous Gentiles."

"Are you going or not?" answered I.

"I will have a kiss now, at all events. If you will give me a kiss, I will leave you to reflect on what I have said, and on the holy revelation of Brother Peter. You had better be reasonable, or we *must* make way with you in some snug way, Sister Boadicea."

"If you do not leave this house, and that speedily," answered I, "I shall make way with you;" and I drew from the bosom of my dress a small pocket pistol of Hubert's, which the *moral tone* of the Mormon society had before that time made a necessary as well as useful weapon of self-defence.

Brother Seth hereupon ran away, as fast as his legs could carry him—home, I suppose, to his nine wives. I pocketed the pistol, which had never yet been loaded. Ah! the Mormon men are the vilest, lowest cowards imaginable.

The former fanaticism has degenerated into mere licentiousness, under the spiritual wife system. The men have become to the last degree demoralized, effeminate, and lazy.

It is the old fable of Hercules at the feet of Onephale[1].

---

1. In Greek mythology, Omphale (not "Onephale" as Bell/Orton writes) was given the hero Heracles (Hercules) as her husband and slave for one year as his punishment for murdering Iphitus. The story has long been famous for casting a great hero in a role of sexual subservience to a woman.

BROTHER SETH PRACTICING ELOCUTION.

CHAPTER VII.

JOURNAL OF BOADICEA.—PART V.

Indignation of Hubert at Holmes' Conduct—Renewal of Holmes'
Pursuit—His Doctrines.

{35} WHEN Hubert returned, he seemed extremely indignant at
what had passed. The possibility of losing me, seemed to revive his
old love, and a short season of peacefulness followed.

After a few days, Brother Seth returned. He had watched the
house and seen Hubert depart. "According to the revelation of the
Prophet Smith," said he, in a loud voice, as I turned impatiently
away, and would not listen to him, "it is lawful and right for you to
become my wife, and live with me; if there be any sin in it, I will
answer for it before God, and you need not trouble yourself about
it at all. Brother Joseph Smith, who has the keys of the kingdom of
heaven, by his spiritual revelation will bind us together, and what-

ever he binds on earth shall be bound in heaven, and whatever he looses on earth shall be loosed in heaven. {36}

"If you will accept of me," continued he, still louder, "you shall be blessed; God shall bless you, and my blessing shall rest upon you. And if you will be led by my will, you will do right and well, for I will take care of you. And if you don't like me in a month or two, you can be free again; you may then like some one else better; but you had better take me *first*." (!!!)

By this time he was purple with shouting to make me hear, for I had stopped my ears to shut out his blasphemies, though I still distinctly heard his roaring voice.

I finally left the room, slamming the door after me. After waiting an hour for me to return, Brother Seth Holmes "retired in disgust."

CHAPTER VIII.

JOURNAL OF BOADICEA.—PART VI.

Serenade of Brother Seth—A Mormon Song.

A few evenings after the second disappearance of Brother Seth, he, on the principle, I presume, that "*music* hath charms to soothe the *savage* breast," gave me an original serenade, of which the intention seemed to be as well to recommend himself to me for *saint-like* and *holy* qualities, as to exercise my mind on the subject of *religion*. The serenade was a *solo*, sung by Brother Seth himself, (outside the door, which I had managed to secure effectually,) and its musical merit was on a parallel with that of the celebrated tune which is supposed to have caused the demise of a certain venerable domestic animal, useful in furnishing "the milk of human—*breakfasts*."

BROTHER SETH'S SERENADE.

A MORMON SONG.[1]

I'm a saint, I'm a saint,
  On the rough world wide;
The earth is my home,
  And my God is my guide.
Up! up! with the truth;
  Let its power bend the knee;
I am sent, I am sent,
  And salvation is free.

I fear not old priestcraft;
  Its dogmas can't awe;
I've a chart for to steer by,
  That tells me the law;
And ne'er as a coward
  To falsehood I'll kneel,
While *Mormon* tells truth,
  Or God's people reveal. {37}

---

1. "I'm a Saint" was written by the Scottish convert John Lyon (1803–1889). It was first published in the *Latter-day Saint Millennial Star* 12, no. 8 (April 15, 1850): 128 and republished in Lyon's book-length collection, *The Harp of Zion* (Liverpool 1853), 171–72. Mayhew reprints it in *The Mormons* (38–39) along with the instruction that it be sung "to the tune of a pirate song by Mr. Henry Russell, called, 'I'm afloat, I'm afloat,' and written by Miss Eliza Cook."

Up! up! with the truth;
　　Let its power bend the knee;
I am sent, I am sent, —
　　Dying Bab'lon, to thee!
I am sent, I am sent,
　　Take this warning, and flee.

The arm of the tyrant
　　Fell terror has spread;
Yet though they oppose us,
　　Their strongholds we'll tread.
What to us is the scorn
　　Of the selfish and vain?
We have borne it before,
　　And we'll bear it again.

The fire-gleaming bolts
　　Of oppression may fall,
And kill off the body,—
　　Death can't us appal.
With heaven above us,
　　And all hell below,
Through the wide world of error
　　Right onward we go.

Come on, my brave comrades;
　　Now's the time you should speak;
The Storm-Fiend is roused
　　From his long dreary sleep:
Our watch-word for safety
　　In Zion shall be;
I am sent, I am sent,—
　　Dying Bab'lon, to thee;
I am sent, I am sent,—
　　Take this warning, and flee.

This astonishing entertainment being ended, Brother Seth took his departure,—not, however, without again trying the door, and endeavoring to effect an entrance.

CHAPTER IX.

JOURNAL OF BOADICEA.—PART VII.

I HERE pause to introduce a portion of the instructions given to women by the Mormon "Fathers, Elders, and Brothers in the Lord," (in the devil!) on the subject of their faith. It is such an answer as I received from Hubert when I asked him what the Morons believed God to be.

THE MORMON BELIEF REGARDING GOD, ANGELS, AND THE FUTURE.[1]

Quest. What is God?

Ans. He is a material organized intelligence, possessing both body and parts. He is in the form of a man, and is, in fact, of *the* {38} *same species;* and is a model or standard of perfection, to which *man* is destined to attain!!! he being the great Father and Head of the Whole Family.

This being cannot occupy two distinct places at once; therefore he cannot be every where present.

(*Remark of author.*—Here we have the omniscience, as well as the omnipresence, of God denied. But the Mormon god is another being.)

Quest. What are angels?

Ans. They are intelligences of the human species. Many of them are the offspring of Adam and Eve—of men, it is said, *being gods or sons of God, endowed with the same powers, attributes, and capacities, that their heavenly Father and Jesus possess!!!!*

The weakest child of God which now exists upon the earth, will possess more dominion, more property, more subjects, and more power and glory than is possessed by Jesus Christ, or by His Father, while at the same time, Jesus Christ and his Father will have their dominions and subjects increased in proportion.

I need make no comment. "Horrors on Horrors!"

---

1. This passage of questions and answers appeared in the *Millennial Star* 6, no. 2 (July 1, 1845): 20. Mayhew considerably shortens it and cites it in *The Mormons*, 48. The version here uses Mayhew's version verbatim, with the exception of exclamation points and italicized words for emphasis.

CHAPTER X.

JOURNAL OF BOADICEA.—PART VIII.

Threats of Brother Seth and Brother Howard.

I WAS left in peace for some little time after this occurrence, when one evening, after I had almost forgotten the existence of Brother Seth, he came across the little grass patch in front of my house, accompanied by Brother Howard, another of the most prominent among the Mormon elders, and a perfect "Saint" in the estimation of all the Mormons.

A singular sensation of fear and loathing nearly overcame me at the sight of these men. I knew the infamous character of the one, and of the other feared the same, because I knew him to be the intimate confederate, agent, jackal, and pander, of the notorious and inconceivably wicked Bernard Yale.

It was as if one of the devil's chiefest fiends had risen from the depths of the lowest hell before me. I felt myself tremble and turn pale, and well I might, for I was alone; it was dark, and growing late, and no human being was within less than a quarter of a mile of my lonely and isolated house. In the midst of my perturbation and alarm, the elders entered my house. Brother Seth surveyed me with a look of sinister delight.

"I have brought Brother Howard," said he, "to bring you to terms, and teach you that we Mormons are not to be trifled with." {39}

"Gently, gently, Brother Seth," interposed Howard; "you mar all by your eagerness and haste; let *me* talk to Sister Boadicea—let *me* open her eyes to the sinfulness of her ways, and show her that she is on the verge of the gulf of perdition. I will cause her to repent and tremble, that she be not cast into uttermost darkness."

"I loathe, detest, and despise your doctrines. I know of what licentiousness, what horrors of iniquity and guilt they serve as cloaks. Why will you torment me? All I ask is, to be left to solitude. Is it not enough that your women have alienated from me my husband's love? Must I, also be subjected to loathsome and guilty proposals?"

"We are aware that Brother Hubert has followed the calls of his religious duties and obligations, and has taken unto himself another love; but he has forborne to bring her here; he goes to her, and is in hopes that you may be induced to assume other ties, and leave the house free to him!" answered Howard.

"That is false, vile traducers!" exclaimed I. "I know that one day his heart will repent, and that he will be again my own dear husband, my own Hubert!" Here I could not help bursting into tears.

Brother Seth seated himself beside me, and attempted to take my hand, which I, however, withdrew, and also pushed my chair to considerable distance from his.

"Verily, sister," said Howard upon this, "you seem to speak as if there was an hope of such foolish conduct and effeminate weakness, on the part of good brother Hubert; but verily, you are mistaken: your better course is to leave him to himself, and by taking unto yourself another companion, to entirely drive him from your memory. We are willing to act mildly in this matter, sister, because of your youth and loveliness; and we would willingly guide you into the paths of righteousness and salvation; think, dearly beloved sister, what would be our feelings when Christ shall have come in person to reign a thousand years on earth, if we behold you, instead of a shining angel, an outcast from glory, weeping and wailing, and gnashing your teeth, like the rebellious Gentiles."

Here I could not help laughing. Brother Howard frowned and turned red.

"Well," answered I, "I do not fear that you will see me in that situation, for the sin of not liking Mr. Holmes; and if this be all you have to say in favor of your religion and your morality, I desire that you will, both of you, quit this place, and leave me to take care of my own soul, and my own salvation."

"What horrible blasphemy!" exclaimed Brother Seth, rolling up his eyes till nothing but the whites were visible: "it makes my blood run cold." Brother Seth hereupon shivered—so did Brother Howard.

"Will you oblige me by withdrawing?" reiterated I.

"No, by no means," answered Brother Howard; "what I wish is a promise from you to listen to Brother Seth's suit, and that you {40} will repent the evil of your ways, and turn from the sinfulness thereof."

"I will never listen to Mr. Holmes' insults," answered I, "and I feel nothing for him but loathing, hatred, and contempt." Here I noticed that the expression of Howard's face grew dark and malignant, and that he exchanged a furtive glance with Holmes.

"Do you know," said he to me, "that we consider it our duty as upholders of a great and honorable sect, to make way with such as contemn our doctrines, despise our words, and threaten us with revolt?"

"I can easily imagine that the presence of such is disagreeable to you; and, therefore, I entreat you, as human beings, to enable me to leave this place. If you will do so, I will never breathe a word of what I have seen and know; but will, for the sake of my unborn child's father, as well as for the sake of freedom, refrain from uttering one word in your dispraise."

As I spoke of "my unborn child" the men started.

"Is this a mere evasion?" said Brother Howard.

"No," answered I, "upon my word of honor as a woman."

"We will leave you then, for a few months, to reflection. If, at the end of that time, your views do not alter, then we shall take other and harsher measures."

With this they left me; and such was the agitation from which I was suffering at their insults and threats, that I could scarcely totter to my room. A violent illness confined me to my bed for a month after this interview, in the midst of which Hubert returned, and behaved with great kindness and affection. This I attributed to a return of love; but it was merely the result of a quarrel with Cephysia.

CHAPTER XI.

JOURNAL OF BOADICEA.—PART IX.

Harem of Bernard Yale—Description of his Wives.

A few days after my recovery, a shooting-match took place at a short distance from my house—at which prizes were awarded to the best pistol shot among the men, and to the best archer among the ladies.

It became necessary, in order to reach the lot where the shooting-match was to take place, that all the ladies should pass my door—which they did on horseback. I had thus an opportunity of seeing assembled together some of the handsomest women in America; among the others, the whole harem of Bernard Yale.

First, in a riding-dress of blue velvet, with a cap of the same, of {42} the "jockey" shape, finished with a gold tassel, and embroidery of the same gold upon her habit, rode a tall blonde. Her features were regular, and her hair, which was of the rare golden blonde description, was remarkably abundant. It fell about her face in glittering and cloud-like curls, displaying her arching and snowy throat as the wind lifted it, and fluttering like a fairy silken banner on the air. The countenance of this woman, though originally it must have been of the order of beauty which is termed angelic, was now almost repulsive, though handsome; for her clear blue eyes shone with a hard, bold and wicked light. Her lips were pale and compressed, and her eyes surrounded with those pink rings, and marked beneath with the livid hues which stamp the drunkard. What a mirror is the human face for reflecting the passions of the soul—especially the female face!

Next rode a woman of that remarkable and always striking order of beauty which combines black lustrous hair with a white complexion, and large oriental eyes with delicate and exquisite features. This face, though of the most noble contour, and accompanied by an elegant form, of that rare and willowy grace which reminds one of the movements of the wild deer, was even more hard and brazen than that of the blonde. The eyes were a hard stare, and the delicate skin was roughened with pink blotches, announcing high living and drunkenness as well.

THE ENGLISH WIFE.

In the appearance of all these women was that reckless *effron-terie*, that hard, bold, brazen look, which the French call *"mauvais air,"* and which invariably marks the woman lost to virtue; that indescribable want of modesty and respectability in the gait, *tournure* and manner, which enables one always to tell a courtesan from a lady, whatever her dress, surroundings and appointments.

The third lady, who rode after this woman, (formerly, I have been told, a distinguished belle of New York,) was a girl of the order of beauty called ches[t]nut blonde. Her large blue eyes, brown hair, with a tinge of auburn—her fair, pale skin and exquisite shape, made her more remarkable than any who accompanied her. Her face was faultless—the features of the Roman type—and wearing a haughty look. Upon a nearer examination, the callous despair, the blank wretchedness of her look, were alone remarkable. She rode as if she particularly wished to be thrown from her horse and killed. I never saw in any living face such utter desolation, such calm, unmoved anguish and despair. She would occasionally strike the reins on her horse's neck, to hasten his speed; and I observed that she shuddered as a coarse oath from one of those who preceded her fell upon her ear. Poor, beautiful, ruined being! Poor Mary Loyd!

The fourth lady was fleshy and not particularly handsome. The only beauty I observed in her was a handsome white hand, which she wore, I observed, ungloved—probably to show its whiteness.

The fifth lady was a wild, sprightly brunette. Her rich dark complexion, with a clear crimson glow, and her sparkling brown {44} eyes, gave her the appearance of unusual health. She laughed as she rode along—showing her pearly and dazzling teeth. I have been told that she was a Spanish woman, who was accused of having poisoned her husband in a fit of jealousy; for which reason she had fled her country. She was one of those whom I should judge that nothing but extreme suffering would lead to see the error of her ways. She appeared to glory in her guilt.

Next rode Cephysia—my rival. I have described her. I noticed that she looked sulky, and did not, as I had anticipated, raise her eyes to my windows as she passed. Perhaps she did not care to see Hubert beside me. For a wonder, he was there.

MARY LOYD.

{43}

THE AMERICAN WIFE.

Next to the brunette rode Bernard Yale. He appeared to be conversing with the brunette. His words were in this wise. As he rode
very slowly I could distinguish what he said.

"God created me, and you, and all mortals, to become gods *like
unto himself. (!)* All human beings were created for this express purpose; that they might increase the intelligence and truth, which
{46} is God, and after they have become gods, even the sons of the
living God, they have the power of peopling earthly TABERNACLES
(the Mormon word for *bodies*) with their spirits, even as they now
have the power to hold spiritual communication with one another."

He rode on, and I could hear no more. From what devil was he
then drawing his strange and diabolic inspiration?

Bernard Yale is a man of tolerable talents and passable address,
without good looks, or that which I should call so; he passes for
"fascinating" among the singularly susceptible persons by whom he

THE SPANISH WIFE.

[NO CAPTION]

is surrounded. He has the faculty of adapting himself to all intellects, all tastes, and all grades. Among the more refined of his associates, he affects the gentleman, but a greater brute and boor, as his wives know to their cost, does not exist. With the ruffian, the outlaw, the murderer, the drunkard, the thief, the forger, this man is hand in glove, boon companion, and instigator, as well as assistant.

The sixth wife followed behind him. She also was not attractive, but seemed quieter and more modest than the others. She did not laugh or swear so loudly.

The seventh and eighth were sisters, both very pretty, rosy English girls. It is no uncommon thing for one man among the Mormons to have three sisters for wives. One man has four own sisters in his harem.

The ninth woman was an Indian; she was handsome; she looked dejected, and did not join in the conversation.

All who followed were handsome, except here and there a coarse, plain, or repulsive face.

Lost! lost! lost! all, save through God's unwearied mercy.

MARY MAXWELL.

CHAPTER XII.

JOURNAL OF BOADICEA.—PART X.

Revolt and Disappearance of Mary Maxwell.

{47} IT was on a quiet morning, while I was seated in my sitting-room, that a woman entered my room, apparently under the influence of great excitement and sobbing with grief.

I dropped my work, rose and went to her, for she appeared about to faint. As I extended my arms, she fell into them, exclaiming, "Save me! save me!"

"From what?" demanded I.

"From hell!" she answered, still under the influence of violent agitation.

In a few moments, however, she grew calmer, and I succeeded in extracting from her that she was named Mary Maxwell, was married, and about to become a mother; that her husband had deserted her for Mona Fernandez, one of the harem of Bernard Yale, (the Spanish woman whom I described in the last chapter,) and that her husband was on that day to bring Mona Fernandez home; that she had {48} rebelled against this, and he had driven her from the house with blows.

Bruises upon her hands and arms, as well as her shoulders, attested the truth of her assertions.

She seemed to fear being pursued. I asked her if any one had followed her; she said "yes," that Yale was "after her."

After much more revealing of horrors, she sank back, appearing to be perfectly exhausted. I myself was trembling with agitation. I feared lest every moment should see Yale enter my house. I was alone, without protection, or weapons of defence.

Mary Maxwell seemed to imagine that I could defend her against Yale. I promised to do my best to protect her; but what, alas! is a woman's arm against the strength of a man? I sat quaking with fear. Mary every moment grew paler and paler. I observed that she appeared to be concealing something in her bosom. On coming nearer to her, I saw that it was a pistol: she drew it forth and showed it to me. "Is it loaded?" asked I.

"It is," she replied; "it is my husband's pistol."

At this moment the door opened. Yale, accompanied by two men, whose faces were covered with masks, entered the room; one of them carried a dark lantern.

Mary had crouched in one corner of the room; I had placed a chair before her, over which, as if carelessly, I threw a large shawl.

"Is one Mary Maxwell, the devil's own child, concealed in this house?" demanded Yale; "if she is, you will do well to give her up; she has already killed one of my men by flinging a knife at him, and I am come to see justice administered upon her."

"You are at liberty to search the premises," answered I, seeing that Yale did not suspect that Mary Maxwell was in the very room where he stood.

"I shall do so," answered he.

Accordingly, he, with the two men, searched the house. I took the opportunity thus offered, of concealing Mary in the garden, thinking that they would hardly search there. It was her own wish.

After a long absence and ineffectual search, Yale again entered the room where I was. "I cannot find her, and yet I am confident that I saw her enter this house."

"You may search it again, if you like," answered I.

"No," grumbled Yale; and he started to depart. As he passed the spot where Mary was crouched in the garden, a white handkerchief, which she had dropped, attracted his attention. he stopped, picked it up, and immediately began to search the garden.

I saw that all was lost; but, determined to defend Mary, I exclaimed, "Run, run, Mary! run!"

She started. The moment I had uttered the words I regretted that I had done so. I saw that she was too weak to run far.

Suddenly she turned, aimed the pistol at Yale, but missing him, shot one of the men, who fell. {49}

With a demoniac shout, Yale and his surviving companion started after her. She disappeared in the direction of the mountains. I sank down into a chair, utterly overcome, and trembling in every limb, but determined to await the event.

CHAPTER XIII.

JOURNAL OF BOADICEA.—PART XI.

AFTER the lapse of quarter of an hour, during which, as I heard no sound, I began to hope that by some miracle, Mary Maxwell had escaped, she suddenly darted into the room, and fell upon the floor, pale, ghastly, and covered with blood. Yale followed after. He entered the room, still accompanied by the masked man, whose companion lay a corpse in my garden, and seeing his victim on the floor, walked towards her.

"Will you go with me?" asked he.

"No," answered the dying woman.

"Then you are done for," said Yale; and deliberately, before my very eyes, in spite of my wild screams for his mercy, he fired at her, and scattered her brains over the floor. I fell down in a death-like swoon. On my recovery, the corpses of Mary Maxwell and Yale's masked companion, Yale himself, and every trace of the bloody murder, had vanished; but for the trampled flowers of my garden, and the ghastly remembrance which will remain in my heart until my dying day, I could have believed it all a dream. Indeed, when I communicated these circumstances to Hubert, and showed him the trampled garden, he told me that I had had an attack of nightmare; and said he did not believe one word I said. Nor could I induce him, by all my representations, to appear, in the least degree, to credit my assertions.

CHAPTER XIV.

JOURNAL OF BOADICEA.—PART XII.

Lawrence Grey's Suicide—Hubert's Sorrow.

As if, in visitation upon Hubert for his indifference to the horrible crime thus perpetrated, one of his own friends, a man to whom he was deeply attached, became one of the victims thereof.

It appeared, that previous to the marriage of Mary Grey to Maxwell, her husband, she had been the sole companion—they being orphans—of her brother, Lawrence Grey.

These two young persons were twins, bearing the most astonishing {50} resemblance to each other; and each seemed to be constantly striving, I have since heard, to surpass the other in affection.

One day Hubert entered the house, accompanied by Lawrence Grey, who looked, in spite of his extreme beauty of appearance, like an exhumated corpse. His eyes were hollow, and glittered with a fierce and frenzied fire; his cheeks were livid; his dark hair matted upon his brow, and his hands trembled convulsively.

"It was here! here, then," exclaimed he, "that Mary died! My poor, poor sister!" and he flung himself upon the floor of the apartment in an agony of grief. {51}

""Come, Grey," said Hubert, "be a man."

"Be a man!" answered Grey; "no, no! Henceforth I am a demon. I live but for one purpose,—to kill Bernard Yale. When that is done, I am ready to depart."

"Calm yourself, Grey, for heaven's sake," answered Hubert; "you do not know"—here he glanced at the windows—"you do not know who may overhear you."

"I care not," answered Grey; "I care not; she is dead—Mary is dead—the world is dead to me;—would to God I were dead too!"

"Will you not consent to live for my sake?" said Hubert, taking his hand with the tenderness of a woman.

"No; I ask but death! speedy death," said Grey; "I care not how soon it comes, or in what shape—but first revenge! revenge! revenge!"

Muttering this, and horrible threats against Yale, the poor maniac left us, and wandered away. On the morrow, a corpse was found floating in the Great Salt Lake; it was that of poor Lawrence Grey.

LAWRENCE GREY.

He had fired at Yale, missed him, been seized by some of Yale's satellites, had escaped from them, and to evade the probable horror of
Yale's revenge, had drowned himself.

Hubert, who discovered the body, wept over it, raved, and called
wildly upon Grey to speak to him. The dead answered not. At last, wild
with grief, poor Hubert bore the body to Yale himself, and, in the most
abject manner, implored him to use his miraculous power, and restore
the dead to life. This man told him "no," that in this case it was impossible; that the spirit within him had "no power over suicides."

Hubert walked away in deep despair, and for the first time, I saw
that his blind faith in Yale was shaken. I profited by this, to implore
him to fly with me: he still sullenly refused.

CHAPTER XV.

JOURNAL OF BOADICEA.—PART XIII.

Birth of Boadicea's Child—Proposal of Hubert to bring another Wife into
His House—Contempt of Boadicea.

. . . . . . At last, after great suffering, I became the happy mother of
a lovely little boy. Those alone who, estranged from all other ties, thus
form a new one, as it were, WITH HEAVEN, can tell what deep joy and
thankfulness were mine. But it was not shared by Hubert. Moody,
gloomy and cold, he scarcely noticed the boy, or spoke to me.

I knew that something was wrong in his mind, which meant
mischief, but the birth of my boy, (whom my still great affection for
his {53} father, induced me to call Hubert,) seemed to nerve me to
any thing. In fact, I thought but little of any thing except my child,
or the lowering looks, the coldness and absence of mind of Hubert
would have soon opened my eyes.

One afternoon, he seated himself beside me, and contrary to his
usual custom, took my hand in his. Surprised by this movement, I
looked up at him, and he began to speak.

"Do you love me, Boadicea?" said he.

"Yes," answered I.

"Sufficiently to sacrifice your own old notions of right and wrong
to my happiness? In fact, sufficiently to sacrifice yourself for me?"

"Yes," answered I, inwardly quaking—for I began to understand
that something dreadful was about to take place—"I love you," reiterated I, "sufficiently to do any thing for your good or happiness."

"Then I will tell you, my dear wife, what I have on my mind. I
wish to take into my house another wife."

I did not move; I did not speak; I did not fall dead—but I felt
as if turned to stone.

"Yes!" continued Hubert, "I feel it to be my duty to take up the
cross of religion, and courageously to follow the example of my
dear brothers in the Lord, for the glory of the Lord. All I ask is your
promise to conduct yourself with propriety and kindness towards
the new-comer." {54}

"For the love of Heaven, do not do this!" answered I. "It will
drive me mad!"

BOADICEA AND HER CHILD.

PRICE AND HIS WIFE

"Oh, no! Recollect it is the custom here. The eyes of the world will soon be opened to the fact that this is indeed the proper way to worship God—by raising up families to His praise. And do you not know that every wife a man takes unto himself is a new angel, whom he leads into heaven; and who becomes thereby sure of heaven, because she has a spiritual husband to lead her there?"

"For Heaven's sake, hush these horrible blasphemies! I cannot and will not hear them!" exclaimed I.

"And is this your love, your gratitude to me, for the affection and kindness which I have shown you; and for my having thus long forborne to bring Cephysia near you—except one single time?"

"Cephysia!" cried I, "is it indeed for that woman that you are about to throw away my pure, earnest and sincere affection? Is it indeed that creature whom you purpose to bring here?"

"It is Cephysia Brown—an excellent, warm-hearted woman; and not one to assail me in this manner, and treat my reasonable and feasible proposition thus. No! she is not selfish; she would willingly suffer another near the throne!"

LIZZIE PRICE IN DISTRESS AT THE TREATMENT OF HER HUSBAND.

"Doubtless *she* would," answered I; "for hers is not pure love like mine."

Was it not too horrible! I knew what was before me. Females, according to the rules and practices of Mormonism, are decidedly inferior beings—created merely for the purpose of ministering to the passions, wants and low propensities of men; and, as Hubert stated, thought to be only admitted to the "communion of the faithful," in this world and the next, through the merits and in consideration of the husband.

The women are treated as but little better than slaves; they are in fact white slaves; are required to do all the most servile drudgery; are painfully impressed with their nothingness and utter inferiority, in divers ways and at all seasons; and are frequently, as in the case of Mary Maxwell, subjected to personal violence and various modes of corporeal punishment.

There was a young woman named Lizzie Price among the Mormons, whose history is a case in point. Her lover was a thorough-bred hunter. He carried his rifle with the grace of a young Apollo. He dressed in rich furs and Indian moccasins, and wore a blanket like a Mexican cloak; but such was the grace of his motions and the beauty of his manly person, that no costume could have been more becoming. In face he resembled Hubert. The wild spirit of adventure alone seemed to stir him until he met with lovely Lizzie Price. Hers was the countenance of one of Raphael's virgins—pure, sad, sweet and holy. He tended her in sickness—she being threatened with consumption. She soon became devotedly attached to him; and, upon his solemn promise not to take another wife until her death, she consented to marry him. In a short time his manner {55}changed. He, like Hubert, frequently absented himself—would threaten and scold her for the merest trifle; and, at last, one day flew into a violent rage at the sight of her grief, when he proposed bringing another wife into the house, and actually beat her—*beat her with his fists*—so violently as to bring on a hemorrhage, which, being repeated, ended her days. She is buried no one knows where. All dead bodies are mysteriously spirited away among the Mormons, and no clue is ever found or sought for the sacred relics of the dead.

{57}I fell ill again with agitation at the dreadful prospect before me. Indeed, having but lately recovered from the pangs of childbirth, I could not bear the agony of mind thus inflicted upon me. I sank under it.

Hubert left me to take care of myself. I should have died but for the kindness of a neighbor, whom I had previously nursed through a long and tedious illness.

DEATH OF LIZZIE PRICE

CHAPTER XVI.

JOURNAL OF BOADICEA.—PART XIV.

Performance of Hubert's second marriage—Introduction of Second Wife—Contempt of Boadicea.

In a few days from this time Hubert was married—"sealed unto" Cephysia Brown. On the second day after the ceremony he brought her to my house. I took no notice of her entrance or of Hubert's. She then attempted to show that *she* was mistress, by laying her hands upon every thing—even some of my clothes, which I was mending. I calmly took them from her, rose with my child, and retired to my room. In that apartment I abode with little Hubert, who grew and thrived; and I never quitted it, except to prepare my frugal meals.

Cephysia immediately appropriated the sitting-room—the ornaments of which she changed to suit her fancy. For some time she did not interfere with me personally. At last, one day, Hubert (before whom she affected extreme mildness and meekness) being absent, she commenced the insults which I saw she was desirous of putting upon me, by snatching from my hands a dish in which I had just placed some vegetables.

I took no more notice than I would have done of the petulance of a child, but continued on my way to my room.

"I want this," she then exclaimed, snatching my shawl from my shoulders.

"Very well," answered I; "take it."

"And this," said she, attempting to unfasten from the bosom of my dress a brooch on which was painted the portrait of Hubert.

"I cannot give you that," answered I; "I value it very much."

"You need not think of him; you need not care for him; he does not care sixpence for you."

"Perhaps not," answered I; "but he is my husband, and I shall always love him."

"Nonsense," answered she; "he is *my* husband now, and I can have you turned out of the house with your brat any day I choose."

"You know perfectly well, Mrs. Brown," answered I, "that in {58} a decent place you would be nothing more than my husband's *mistress*—that any true and righteous law will uphold me as his only and legitimate wife. But it matters not. I am content to bear what Providence has visited upon me, doubtless for some good and wise purpose. All I ask is that you will let me alone. I shall not either address you or interfere with you or Hubert in any wise."

"But I hate the sight of your chalk-white face," answered Cephysia; "and out of the house you shall march, sooner or later. I shall tell Hubert what you have been saying, every word of it, and that you called me his mistress. Mistress, indeed! I'm his *wife*."

With this I left her, for she had, by this time, worked herself up into a violent rage, and looked so red and angry, that I was quite afraid of her.

Things continued for some time in this way, made worse, however, by the scowling countenance with which Hubert looked at me, whenever, by any accident, he encountered me; and by his encouraging Cephysia's impertinence and contemptuous conduct in every imaginable way.

I bore up as well as I could, endeavoring to console myself in the sweet society of my lovely infant, and by the reflection that, painful as was my lot, it was Paradise in comparison to that of many other women in the settlement, for Hubert had never yet laid his hand in violence upon me.

Every day I grew paler, feebler, and thinner, for the desertion of Hubert, and his ill-humors were breaking my heart. I loved him as I can never love any other. He was the first I have ever loved—the last, the only one.

Cephysia had now appropriated to her own use, and kept locked, all the other apartments, except the kitchen. During my short absences from my own room, she managed to introduce herself into it, and appropriated, also, all my handsomest clothes, as well as the coveted brooch.

I said nothing—only it was with a feeling resembling joy, that I one evening observed that Hubert started back in great displeasure, and frowned darkly, at seeing her dressed in a dress which it had once given him pleasure to see me arrayed in.

He spoke to her about this. I do not know what he said, but that evening he came into my room, bringing with him all the dresses of which Cephysia had robbed me, and also the brooch. Bending over me, he fastened the brooch in the bosom of my dress, clasped me fervently in his arms, kissed me several times with great warmth, and withdrew from the room, after placing the dresses upon a chair.

A MORMON FAMILY.

CHAPTER XVII.

JOURNAL OF BOADICEA.—PART XV.

Second Wife (Cephysia) Ill-treats Boadicea and Little Hubert—Attempts
to Poison Boadicea.

{59} IT was about four months after she had been brought into
my house, that I observed that Cephysia surveyed me with scowling brows. As I passed her on the stairs, she pretended to trip, and
her heavy weight falling against me, caused me to fall and severely
bruise my head. In a moment I was covered with blood from the
severe gash inflicted. Faint, giddy, tottering, and utterly miserable, I
managed to reach my room.

In the evening, Hubert, observing that my brows were bound
up, asked me what was the matter. I told him. He seemed very
angry, and sending for Cephysia, made her ask my pardon, and
promise never to molest me more.

She sullenly promised, but the "lurking devil in her eye," for-
bade me to believe that she did so with sorrow or sincerity, or with
the remotest intention of keeping her promise.

After a few days, I observed that she seemed, more than ever be-
{60} fore, to notice my child; at last she asked me to let her take it.
I replied that I did not wish to trust him out of my arms, as he was
delicate, and she was not accustomed to children.

She went away pouting. After a while she came back, and
snatched the child, (who was then in a good deal of pain, and cry-
ing in consequence,) from my arms.

"I'll teach the brat to yelp and yell in that style!" said she, and
she struck the little creature a violent blow.

I took him from her; "What!" said I, as calmly as I could, "would
you commit the crime of murder? Would you kill my child? Go,
woman, go, and the Lord have mercy upon you, and cast out the
devil which has you in possession." With this, I took her by the arm
and led her from the room, the door of which I locked.

I heard nothing more from her for several days; I found that the
little Hubert was not injured by her violence; in fact, I think that
then her design was more to anger me, which she had not yet succeeded in doing, than to injure him. She entered my room a week
after this, wearing a smile on her face, and holding in her hand a
plate. On the plate was a rich cake, of which she invited me to take
a slice, saying that she had made it for Hubert.

I unsuspiciously took a piece of it, which, however, I refrained
from eating then, as I was not hungry at the time. I had one pet in
my room—a bird, whose brilliant plumage had induced Hubert to
catch it. He had brought it home to me, and constructed a cage,
in which I still kept "Favorite," as I called the bird, for I prized and
cherished it for Hubert's dear sake.

I know not what induced me to crumble the cake in my hand,
and to feed my bird with it, but, in a few moments after swallowing
the crumbs, with which I fed it, the little creature fluttered from
its perch, gave a convulsive struggle, and fell dead in the bottom of
the cage. I stood amazed, horrified, and trembling: that Cephysia
Brown was a bad-tempered, abandoned, violent woman, I knew;
that she was a murderess I had not as yet believed.

Willing to convince myself further, I fed one of the animals in the
yard, a hunting dog, with the remains of the cake: it expired instantly.

I now determined to leave the house,—knew not where to go.
The neighbor whom I had nursed was a poor Indian woman, very

[NO CAPTION]

old and infirm, named "Fawn Fleet." She was my only friend in the whole settlement. To her I determined to go. I accordingly packed up the few articles in my possession, in readiness to depart upon the earliest absence of Hubert.

The lovely little Hubert grew and thrived, despite my sorrows. I spent many a happy hour, in spite of them, over the little darling's cradle. I never tired of holding him in my arms, of dressing him, bathing his rosy limbs, working on his tiny garments, and curling the tendrils of his clustering hair.

There is no such sweet society as that of a little child. A mother {61} sees many indications of intelligence, which will not strike any eye but a mother's—many a beauty which, perhaps, may exist only in her imagination, but which makes her darling the delight of her eyes, and the pride of her heart. So passed the long days: I felt only too grateful to God for my precious charge. To escape, to fly, to reach the States, and establish myself with my boy in a Christian society, was my sole dream, my sole purpose in existence. I thought of that alone, and I felt sure that once there, old ties would renew themselves in Hubert's mind, and that he would soon join me.

BOADICEA CONFIDING IN FAWN FLEET.

CHAPTER XVIII.

JOURNAL OF BOADICEA.—PART XVI.

{62} I ACCORDINGLY left Hubert's house one evening, during one of his absences. To my surprise and sorrow, however, I found "Fawn Fleet," to whom I hastened, very ill. I nursed her faithfully, and after I had succeeded in producing some little change for the better, a relapse took place, and she became feverish; the fever increased, she grew delirious, and, on the tenth day after my arrival, she died.

Being very ill myself, I determined now to return for a short time to Hubert's house, hoping that he might still be absent therefrom. When I arrived, I found that he had not yet returned. He had recently become an important person among the Elders and Saints, and would very often absent himself whole weeks without appearing, and would account for these absences, by saying to Cephysia, that he had been attending to "religious matters."

She would rec[ei]ve him sulkily, grumble a little, and no more would be said. Heaven only knows with what dark and hideous mysteries this time was occupied. I know only that each day appeared to harden him more against me, the boy, and even Cephysia, of whom he now appeared heartily tired. Cephysia now renewed her ill-treatment of me. There was no unkindness, no insult, no low language, no unwomanly slight, to which, in my then feeble and wretched state of health, she failed to subject me. {63}

I endeavored to bear up against this, but it was with a desolate soul, a drooping and heavy heart. I pitied Cephysia as much as I despised her. Once a beautiful girl, naturally strong passions and sinful tastes had led her away from the path of rectitude and virtue.

The path of sin is ever strewn with thorns, and I doubt whether Cephysia was not far, far more utterly wretched, withal, than I, for *she* knew that in her heart she was not only an adulteress, but also nearly a murderess. Poor woman, self-condemned, self-tortured, self-hating!

I continued to nurse my little darling, and Cephysia seemed gloomier and more sullen every day, but no longer approached, or in any way attempted to molest me. Of this I felt glad, for my heart was very heavy. I thought that my last hours were approaching, such was the feebleness I experienced, and I had the very natural wish to die where my few happy days had been spent, and in Hubert's abiding place.

In the mean time, the strangeness of Cephysia's behavior attracted my attention. She was gloomy, and very melancholy. I noticed that she ate opium, under the intoxicating effects of which, combined with the stimulant of liquors, she would talk in a strange, wild strain. Once I asked her, while suffering, as I could see she was, from one of these melancholy attacks, if she did not wish to fly to the States.

"No, no!" she exclaimed; "the Prophet Smith hath declared, that not very many years will elapse, before the whole of the United States will present a horrible scene of general bloodshed, such as has no parallel in the history of nations. Earthquakes, hail, pestilence, and famine, will sweep the wicked Gentiles who abide there from off the face of the earth, 'to open and prepare the way for the lost tribes of Israel.'"

"Do you believe—can you really believe this?" said I.

"Yes, it is the truth of revelation," answered Cephysia; "none, none shall be spared among the blinded and damned generation of the Gentiles. We alone—we people of the Lord, and people of the chosen Zion, we alone shall be saved out of the fire that forever burneth!"

"What a horrible doctrine!" exclaimed I.

MORMON COURTSHIP.

"Yes, yes! I feel! I see! I know!" shouted the woman, whose every word and gesture announced insanity. "I know that we, we shall live and reign with Christ a thousand years in glory!"

"Do you believe the Mormon faith will indeed save your soul?" asked I.

"I do," answered she; "yes, yes! such is the saving power of that faith, that if I had committed a murder every day of my life, committed all possible earthly sins, I should arise, through that faith, at the last trump; and my spirit be restored to my body, {64} because I have received the holy and perfect baptism which cleanseth from all possible contamination of sin."

She spoke with a kind of exaltation; indeed, I believe that her sinful life and present habits were, even at that time, while she was still a young and handsome woman, driving her mad.

"Whom the gods would destroy, they first make mad."[1]

---

1. This line, "whom the gods would destroy they first make mad," is often attributed, incorrectly, to the Greek playwright Euripides. The phrase "those whom the gods wish to destroy they first make mad" appeared as an uncredited "ancient proverb" in Rev. William A. Scott's book, *Daniel, a Model for Young Men: A Series of Lectures* (New York: R. Carter & Brothers, 1854).

CHAPTER XIX.

JOURNAL OF BOADICEA.—PART XVII.

Symptoms of Consumption—Brother Howard Wishes Boadicea to become one of his Wives.

{65} I CONTINUED ill, though I still managed to keep about; but the symptoms of latent consumption were developing themselves in my system. That is the disease of which the broken-hearted generally die.

Night-sweats, a constant pain in my breast, cold feet, an occasional hemorrhage, the pallor almost of death itself, succeeded by hectic fever, emaciation, slight however, and sleeplessness, were gradually enfeebling me. The secret of all this was a breaking heart.

Hubert observing this, grew kinder. I think that he judged that my days would be but few; I thought so then.

A broken heart! How frequently women—aye, and men, too, die of this!

It is less violent grief, very often, than the fact that the enthusiasm of life is over, gone! After one deception, and the falling to earth of all one's most glorious and loveliest hopes, that enthusiastic belief which makes life, by its fair illusions, a dream of bliss, and earth a paradise for a little time, being gone forever, a settled, calm despair, often unsuspected by outward eyes, takes possession of the spirit, the rest of existence is but a weary exile from the hoped-for rest of heaven, which neither duty nor faith can brighten to the "light of other days."[1] "A wounded spirit, who shall bear?"[2]

While I was still ill and languishing, Brother Howard came to the house. This time he came not as a suitor for Brother Seth Holmes; but to plead his own guilty cause, and to induce me to become one of his wives.

He commenced his conversation, as usual, with what is called "religious" cant,—an expression which, by the by, contradicts itself;

---

1. "The Light of Other Days" is a poem by the Irish poet and playwright Thomas Moore (1779–1852).

2. "The spirit of a man will sustain his infirmity; but a wounded spirit who can bear?" Proverbs 18:14 (KJV).

for religion, true religion, has nothing to do with *cant* in any shape or way. After a little of that style of discourse, he thus continued:

"I think, beloved and lovely Sister Boadicea, that where a perfect adaptation exists between two persons, such as I am confident exists between you and I, it is perfectly accordant with our pursuit of happiness on earth to adapt ourselves eternally, and devote ourselves solely, to each other. With a being like yourself, beautiful Boadicea," continued he, "the heart would be lulled into an everlasting and felicitous repose, for you fill the whole mind with {66} the poetical ideal of womanhood, while your elegance and accomplishments, the elevated tone of your mind, and the perfection of your manner, leave nothing further to be desired. All other beings fall short of the exalted ideal which you present—all ideas formerly received are forever forgotten at the first glance of your inthralling eyes, your lovely and inspiring countenance. Never, never can I forget the effect which the first sight of you produced in me,—never, if you will accept me for your husband, will I, like the tasteless Hubert, wander from your side, or bring another being into the sacred cycle wherein you shall dwell. Be but mine! mine!" (here brother Howard, *the Saint!* fell on his knees before me,) "be but mine, adored one, and no destiny, no creed, shall ever part us."

This might have had some effect upon a person not strengthened as I was against temptation, by my attachment to Hubert, for Brother Howard was rather a handsome man, and spoke with much enthusiasm and apparent sincerity; but I regarded it simply as folly, for I knew by Hubert's inconstancy, how men can

> "Give countenance to their speech,
> With almost all the holy vows of heaven."[3]

I was about to leave Howard in indignant horror, but he angrily rose and detained me.

"Since, madam," said he, "you refuse to listen to peaceful and kind proposals, I will endeavor to make you sensible of your folly by other means; and I now apprise you, that if you do not accept my proffer, your life is not one moment safe: at any time a chance

---

3. Boadicea paraphrases Ophelia's words to Polonius that Prince Hamlet "hath given countenance to his speech, my lord / With almost all the holy vows of heaven." *Hamlet*, Act I, scene 3, lines 113–14.

shot may reach you, and who will suspect, who will dare say that I am guilty?"

"I care not what you do, what you say; but for my child, my life is indifferent to me. I will never listen to you, and I advise you to go your ways."

Howard rose, muttering threats between his teeth, and left the room.

CHAPTER XX.

JOURNAL OF BOADICEA.—PART XVIII.

Scorn of Boadicea—She Expresses her Horror of the Mormon Doctrines.

In vain did Howard pursue me—in vain did he in every way plead his loathsome and guilty suit. I was proof against his pleadings. His voice fell upon my ear as water upon a rock, and my heart remained faithful to my beloved Hubert.

I felt, for all he said—his cant, his hypocrisy, his high-flown sen- {67} timent, the absence of all principle, or moral tone in the very character and mind of the man—a most thorough and unmitigated contempt.

Persons may learn to love one whom they have hated, but never one whom they *despise;* and Howard I most thoroughly despised as a hypocrite and liar.

I paid very little attention to these threats, with which he had sought to alarm me during our last interview; and, indeed, in my own heart, thought them no more than idle threats meant to alarm me into accepting him. I afterwards found out my error.

Upon Howard's presenting himself at my house again, I found that he had an ally in Cephysia. She not only wished to bring me to her own level, to make me as impure as herself, but also wished me to leave her in possession of the house, in order that she might be queen "of all she surveyed."[1]

Indeed I have little doubt but that, through hatred, jealousy and avarice, women have misled as many women as men have ruined.

I took occasion, in the presence of Cephysia and of Howard, to express my unbounded contempt of the Mormon association. "This place," said I, "is a pandemonium where vice runs riot. It would rival Hades in its motley crew of sinners. Whom do I see held up as Saints, and saluted as 'Fathers,' 'Brothers' and 'Elders' of the Church?—whom but gamblers, murderers, drunkards and blacklegs? Here is a safe retreat, a welcome home, for the forger and the horse-thief. Your very laws and foundations are the most

---

1. An allusion to "The Solitude of Alexander Selkirk" by William Cowper (1731–1800): "I am monarch of all I survey, / My right there is none to dispute; / From the centre all round to the sea, / I am lord of the fowl and the brute."

MORMONS DISGUISED AS INDIAN SPIES.

abandoned impurity. How shall ye prosper? If you abide for a time, it is because the hand of the Lord is stayed. But, like Sodom and Gomorrah, your day will come. The sins tolerated here cry out to God for vengeance; and it will one day come. I shall live, perhaps, to see justice visited upon Bernard Yale, your Elder! who, in my presence, shot at, and killed, a defenceless woman—Mary Maxwell!" I saw that Cephysia and Howard were surprised; they said nothing, however. "Yes!" continued I; "mothers and daughters here strive against each other for the preference of that man—dipped as he is in the blood of many victims. You can remember Lawrence Grey. I see your elders wander about, loathing those they have already ruined, and forever seeking a prey among the unappropriated of the women around me; while those thus left match with their seducers in iniquity and play the same shameless game. What horrors are permitted without a word! for I know well that these husbands are the masters, the bashaws, the sultans of many of their neighbors' wives—who, provided they acquiesce in that arrangement—are in all things, except mere publicity, the same to them as the own true and real wife of each and every one."

I saw the Cephysia and Howard were surprised. They interchanged glances of secret understanding; and, after a time, went out, arm-in-arm.

{69} When they were gone I reflected that perhaps I had been imprudent to speak thus; and yet I did not alarm myself much about it. I knew that, as the saying is, I should "not die till my time came," and so I dismissed all recollection of Howard, with the secret prayer that I might be permitted to reach the States ,and, by my pen, put forth the horrors I had witnessed, in order to swell the outcry for the speedy destruction of such a hell of vice as the Mormon colony, and do my "little all" towards arresting further horrors.

CHAPTER XXI.

JOURNAL OF BOADICEA.—PART XIX.

Ball of the Mormon Elders—Attempt at Boadicea's Life—Agitation of
Hubert—Rage of Cephysia—Imprudent Language of Hubert.

At about this time a ball was given by the Mormon Elders—at
which I had a desire to be present. I therefore went in company
with Hubert, and Howard escorted Cephysia.

Festoons of evergreen adorned the Mormon flags. At the end of
the hall was a raised dais. This was intended for the seat of honor,
and was to be occupied by Bernard Yale, the saint (!!!), and his
favorite Sultana, or Elect Lady, as she is called. There were also seats
placed lower down, for such women as had formerly been favorites.

There was excellent music. Many of the pieces performed were
by Strauss.

The Elders, or Lords, entered the room with their last favorites on
their arms. There were a great number of young bachelors, who flirt-
ed, danced, and paid the usual attentions to the belles of the evening.

Poor women! poor favorites! poor wives! "A woman,"—says one
who has made the Mormons the subject of his criticism,—"cannot
live out half her days among the Mormons; for, if her husband
has not *already* tired of her faded beauty, and deprived her of her
rights, she is in the constant fear that he will bring home a fairer
one; and she suffers as acutely in suspense as if he had already done
as others do: turned her from the best apartment in the house, and
compelled her to do the drudgery of her rival, and actually to be
her servant—while the brute has forgotten, in looking on her pale
cheek and dim eye, that the beauty she brought to him at the altar,
has been freely given at the shrine of maternity; and, though she has
lost it forever, their children bear it in threefold perfection; for it has
not been wasted, only transferred.[1]

I was quietly gazing at the ceremonies of the ball, when, opposite
{70} me, at one of the windows, I observed the face of Howard, who,
in the early part of the evening, had quitted Cephysia. If I had been
turned to stone upon the spot, I could not have been more unable

---

1. This passage is listed nearly verbatim from Orvilla S. Belisle's novel, *The
Prophets; or, Mormonism Unveiled* (Philadelphia: Wm. White Smith, 1855), 296.

to move. I saw him raise a rifle, rest it on his shoulder, take aim at me, and then he deliberately fired. The shot missed me, and pierced the brain of the Spaniard—Mona Fernandez—who was waltzing a little way beyond. With a loud cry her partner dropped her, and she fell dead upon the floor of the ball-room—her brains spattering the garments of the women near her. It would be impossible to depict the consternation which ensued. Most of the women rushed from the hall; and Hubert, disengaging himself from Cephysia, who attempted to hold him back, rushed to me, caught my falling form in his arms, and, as I lost all recollection, I could hear him calling me fond names amidst the execrations of Cephysia.

When I returned to my senses, I saw Cephysia still looking at me with an expression of malignant rage—while Hubert, apparently forgetful of her presence, knelt before me—still wearing a distracted and anxious face.

I overheard Hubert muttering to himself threats against Howard. Trembling at his imprudence in speaking thus in this crowded assemblage, I entreated him to be silent—and, even as he continued thus to speak, placed my hand upon his lips. He kissed my hand, and was silent; but, alas! it was too late. I saw that Seth Holmes, who stood near, had overheard him; for he gave me a threatening look, muttered something to himself, and left the ball-room.

In spite of Cephysia's rage, Hubert supported my tottering steps to the door, and accompanied me home. Cephysia arrived soon after. She came to the door of my room, and finding that Hubert was seated beside me, broke out into the most violent and unrestrained abuse—until Hubert ordered her to go to her own room; then she began to abuse him; whereupon he rose angrily from his seat—took her by the arm, led her to her room, and locked her in it.

He now returned to me, and seated himself beside me, extracted from me by his questions, the whole matter concerning Howard, his visits, his courtship (so to speak), and his threats against my life. He trembled and quivered with rage several times, during my recital, and bounded up from his seat every now and then, uttering the most appalling threats against Howard's life, calling him "coward," "villain," "dastard," "dog," and many other very appropriate names.

I now endeavored to calm him, but it was a long time ere I could succeed in doing so. For hours, he still paced the room; I could hear him say, "no use, my God! no use"—"fenced in as he is!"—"could I but meet him alone!"—"no satellite near!" &c., &c., from which I judged that he was really unable to attack Howard, without the interference of some one of his agents and abettors.

REPENTANCE OF HUBERT.

CHAPTER XXII.

JOURNAL OF BOADICEA—PART XX.

Repentance of Hubert—He proposes Flight—Cephysia overhears—
Swedenborgianism versus Mormonism.

{71} HUBERT was now a changed man. Nothing could surpass the devotion with which he attended upon me. He watched my every motion, anticipated my least wish. He ordered Cephysia to return to her former abode, and upon her stating her inability to do so, he found her a residence, which he comfortably furnished, and in which he placed her. She left the house with threats.

There is a certain innate propriety about the generality of women, even those who lead lives not strictly virtuous, which will restrain them from using low and indelicate language; a fastidiousness of manner, so to speak; but Cephysia, like all the more lost and wicked of the Mormon women, was extremely low and coarse, as well in her tastes as in her manner of expressing herself; though she could affect nicety and play the lady upon occasion, the stamp of *vulgarity*, innate vulgarity, was indelible.

It fills me, even now, with amazement, to think that so low, so {72} illiterate and unrefined a woman should ever have influenced an intellect so powerful, tastes so cultivated, and a mind so refined as Hubert's naturally was. For a time, by what fascination I know not, she had obscured his better nature, planted weeds where flowers had grown, and if her influence had continued longer, would have transformed a noble being into a brutal clod.

But this was not permitted. A return of happiness,—a summer smile on the dreary winter of my life, was permitted me; a short return of happiness, ere it bade me farewell, I fear, forever.

I have often thought, in perusing the lives of great men, that the greater part of them appear to have been temporarily under the control of some ignoble and vile female influence, under which influence the foulest stains have marred the history of their lives. St. Anthony was tempted by the devil in *female* shape, be it remembered.

Many will, doubtless, think, if any find it worth while to peruse this little history of suffering, that I was weak to take Hubert back thus, without one word of reproof, or reference to the past, yet I did so, and I have never repented it. We are parted now, but it is by the parting of the All-Powerful Hand, and I have to console me the blessed recollection that I made Hubert's last days happy. In that remembrance dwells my only comfort.

One evening, as we sat in our little garden, Hubert proposed to me to fly from the Mormon state with him and our boy, (whom he now appeared to idolize,) to reach the States, and live out the remainder of our days in an honorable manner.

It may be imagined with what joy I consented. We arranged our plan of flight. I noticed an occasional rustling of the bushes near us, and once I almost started from my seat at the noise of breath drawn pantingly near me, but when we searched the bushes we found no one. As we rose to leave it, however, which we did somewhat abruptly, I saw the black eyes of Cephysia, glittering with fiendish light, beneath a small tree a few paces from us.

I pointed her out to Hubert, who approached her."One word of what you have heard, woman," said he, "one word of it to the Elders, and I give you my everlasting curse."

"I care neither for you nor your curses," answered Cephysia; and she disappeared, uttering the most horrible blasphemies.—I pause here to remark, that I have heard ignorant persons, discussing the "Mormon question," say, "Oh, they are something like the Swedenborgians (!!!); they don't believe in hell, and they do believe in spirits, and such things."

Now nothing could be more different (as all enlightened persons, even of opposite religious sects, will uphold me in saying) from Mormonism than the doctrines of Emmanuel Swedenborg. The former is the creed of the devil; the latter that of the Lord. I know enough of Swedenborg to know this. His doctrines enjoin and inculcate, {73} *above all things, a pure life.* To commit adultery is, according to Swedenborg, *"to admit the devil."*

It scarcely needs that I should state this; the well-read of every sect have handled the enlightened doctrines of Swedenborg, and know that what I here assert is *true.*[1]

I entered the house disturbed in spirit. Hubert laughed at my fears.

---

1. Emanuel Swedenborg (1688–1772) was a Swedish philosopher and mystic whose views on the trinity, the afterlife, and the spiritual importance of good works paralleled some of the beliefs of nineteenth-century Mormonism. A connection between Mormonism and Swedenborgism was suggested by Maria Ward in her 1855 anti-polygamy novel, *Female Life Among the Mormons,* 17.

CHAPTER XXIII.

JOURNAL OF BOADICEA.—PART XXI.

Hubert is strangled—Discovery of his Body through Cephysia.

I NOW approach that part of my history which I tremble to write—it is so horrible; and yet I must, I will nerve myself to write it out; for I am but one of many who have suffered misery,—even such misery as my wrung heart has borne.

Hubert left me one lovely morning, promising to return soon, his countenance glowing with health and animation—every thing speaking in his gait, his manner, his words, his looks—of love, hope, and life.

Little did I think then, when his lips pressed mine, as he retraced his steps to kiss his boy, that I looked upon his living face for the last, *last* time.

How sad seems the future—how dark—how hopeless! for my poor husband, whom his very faults could never estrange from my heart, sleeps, alas! with the hidden dead.

I know not what presentiment of evil made me weary soon of my work, and I restlessly wandered about from room to room, occasionally running to the window, fancying I heard Hubert's voice. I *never* heard it more.

While, having at last seated myself again, I was quieting my boy to sleep, Cephysia entered my room. It struck me that she was lividly pale, but the second time I looked I fancied it might be the candle-light, night having set in.

"Come with me," said she, in a hollow and fearful voice; "come to your lord and master."

"What mean you?" answered I. "Where is he?"

"If you would see him alive, come with me. He has embraced you, my white lily," continued she, using the pet name by which Hubert sometimes called me; "he has embraced you for the last time."

"In heaven's name, tell me what you mean!" exclaimed I, clasping my hands in entreaty.

"Come and see," answered Cephysia. {74}

I laid my sleeping infant down, and as I carefully arranged the clothes about his little form, I noted the wild, wicked eyes of

Cephysia fixed upon me, and then upon him, with so malignant an expression that I shuddered involuntarily.

I did not attach much importance to her wild words, and wilder manner, for I had long looked upon her as insane. I followed her, however, to some distance from the house, and I noticed that the earth seemed roughened and broken, as if by the tread of heavy feet.

We still continued to walk on, and a heavy dread began to overpower me. Scarcely could I drag myself along. I seemed as if under the influence of some hideous nightmare. The form of Cephysia, as it looked up beside me, (she was a tall, as well as a large woman,) seemed to assume diabolic outlines and weird proportions.

We continued to walk until I heard voices muttering. As I looked up, I saw a group of persons assembled together; each of them held a dark lantern, and in the moonlight their faces were distinctly visible. Two of the group were Howard and Holmes.

Over what did they bend, think you, with eyes glaring with malignant and fiendish satisfaction? It was above the corpse of Hubert, the dead body of my husband, strangled by their demon-hands!

At first I did not discern Hubert's face, but presently the lantern of Howard was turned round, and the light flashed upon his upturned brow.

"Dead, stone dead!" said Howard.

In one instant I darted from Cephysia, who had held my arm as in a vice. I flung myself into the midst of the conspirators.

"Leave him to me, leave him to me!" cried I. "You have killed him, you have killed my husband; your hate is satisfied against us both; leave his cold corpse with me!"

With one accord they rose; Howard dropped the body; they fled one and all, leaving Cephysia alone with me, and the dead body of the dearest being on earth, to his poor, heart-broken wife.

I imagined that he might not be quite, quite dead! In vain I loosened the cords from his throat—in vain did I chafe his hands, and kiss his stony and clay-cold brow. He was dead!—he was dead!

CHAPTER XXIV.

JOURNAL OF BOADICEA.—PART XXII.

Horrible and malignant Exultation of Cephysia—Horror of Boadicea—
Her swoon—Hemorrhage of the Lungs.

Looking up, I saw Cephysia; to the hour of my death I can never forget her face. Hate was satisfied against me. Hubert was dead, {75} and upon her countenance was de[p]icted malignant and devilish satisfaction.

Then she exclaimed, "Now we are even—the white lily and the dark lady stand on the same level now. The dead is neither yours nor mine. Yes!" continued she, "he sought me; and of all the world, him only have I loved, him alone, him alone! You robbed me of his heart when at last it was all mine; and I hate you with an undying hate. To death will I pursue you, for you have driven me mad! mad! mad!"

And tearing her hair, howling, and wailing, the maniac fled from me out of the country, leaving me petrified with speechless horror.

I fell beside my dead husband in a swoon. I found myself, on awaking, at home. A neighbor hearing my child cry, had, in passing, entered, and procured assistance. I lay upon my bed—beside me, the corpse of Hubert, the face veiled; and a handkerchief which covered my mouth was saturated with blood from a copious hemorrhage of the lungs.

The kind neighbor, Mrs. Munroe, an old lady, whom I had known in the States, and an excellent woman, was walking up and down the room, wringing her hands.

"How horrible!" said she to me. "How did all this happen?"

I could not speak to tell her. I fell back in a long, death-like trance, from which I awoke to a delirious fever, which lasted a month.

Mrs. Munroe watched over me and my child, as a mother might have done. I know nothing of what happened within the month—it is a long blank in my life.

ILLNESS OF LITTLE HUBERT.

CHAPTER XXV.

JOURNAL OF BOADICEA.—PART XXIII.

Despair of Boadicea—Illness of Little Hubert—Cephysia Poisons the
Little Hubert.

I AWOKE to despair. A dull, gloomy, settled despondency weighed
continually upon my heart, when I began, as the expression is, to
realize my fate. Alone, except for a helpless child, a widow indeed,
friendless, surrounded by bitter enemies, and the object of the in-
veterate hatred of an insane woman.

How heavily the icy hand of Death presses upon the heart!
Death, the *great reality*, which not even the atheist, the infidel, can
deny; the solemn, mysterious parting for that

—"bourn from which no traveler returns."[1]

All other afflictions seem trivial in comparison to this. Illness,
mental suffering, poverty, distress of all kinds, may be borne with
{76} cheerfulness and resignation, but the dreary separation of death,

---

1. From Hamlet's famous "To be or not to be" soliloquy in Act III, scene
1, death is described as "the undiscovered country from whose bourn / No
traveler return" (lines 80–81).

the dark uncertainty which makes the spirit faint lest the parting be for all eternity, forever and ever; this is, indeed, the sorrow of sorrows.

I often wonder to see how callous it is possible for persons, even the most fondly attached to each other, to become, alluding with calmness to the dead and gone. Their trust must be great.

My heart seems to me the grave of Hubert, and ever and anon rings in my ears the wild song of poor, crazed Ophelia.

> "And will he not come again?
> And will he not come again?
>   No, no; he is dead;
>   Go to thy death-bed,
> He never will come again.

> "He is dead and gone,
>   And we cast a weary moan,
> And peace be with his soul."[2]

In the midst of this dull, heavy sorrow, as if purposely to rouse me to exertion, my little boy fell ill. Despite my care, he rapidly grew worse, moaning and tossing with fever, and continually tortured with pain.

The lovely creature had twined himself about my very heart-strings. I loved him next to Hubert, but with another love; that deep, intense, unutterable feeling—"a mother's love."

Perhaps there is no love so tender, so deep, so earnest, so unalterable.

I would cheerfully, willingly have died to secure happiness to my boy. To a mother it seems nothing to die for her child. {77}

Little Hubert still grew worse. It was impossible for me to procure good medical assistance, and I was too young and inexperienced to act with promptness and discrimination; and even had I been better informed as regarded the illnesses of children, it would have prolonged his life but a little while, for he, too, my poor darling child, was doomed. Yes! Have I not reason to hate the Mormons, since their hellish doctrines ultimately produced the death of both my husband and child?

One day Cephysia entered my house. She seated herself beside me, though I recoiled, and offered her no welcome, and began talking in a wild, rambling manner, now common to the poor, frantic being.

---

2. *Hamlet*, Act IV, scene 1, line 160.

"Let me take the baby," said she, at last; and I, fearing to refuse her, let her take him; "I have brought him some medicine to quiet him," said she, and immediately administered some by pouring down his throat a large draught, from a small bottle which she held in her hand.

"What is that, Cephysia?" exclaimed I, snatching the infant from her.

"Nothing but a cordial," said she; "don't disturb yourself—he'll soon be quieted now."

It never occurred to me that she was giving the infant anything that would injure him, though I should have feared it, from her attempt to poison me.

Presently my infant, still faintly moaning, closed his eyes, and after a few moments fell into a deep and tranquil sleep. From that deep sleep he never woke—the she-devil, Cephysia, had drugged him with a heavy dose of laudanum!

On the morrow finding that he still slept, I sought for her every where. At last I found her crouched beside the place where, through my entreaties, the Mormon authorities had interred my husband.

Upon my resolutely demanding of her what she had given my child, she exclaimed, "Laudanum enough to kill you!"

Then, with a loud cry of maniacal exultation and triumph, she arose and bounded away.

DEATH OF BOADICEA'S CHILD.

CHAPTER XXVI.

JOURNAL OF BOADICEA.—PART XXIV.

Death of Little Hubert.

{78} IN vain did I use every means in my power to rouse my poor baby; the drug had been too powerful; the little innocent being's short life was ended. He and his father are now perhaps united, but I am all alone.

Mrs. Munroe endeavored to assist me. Our utmost efforts were of no avail. The and of God had indeed fallen heavily upon me. I cannot dwell longer upon this unhappy time. I grow cold and trembling when I think upon it.

I know not what angelic influence prevented me, distracted and heart-broken as I was, from ending my misery by suicide, but it was not suffered me to soil my soul by that deadly and rebellious sin.

Yet what a fearful temptation it is to the heart-broken! The rest seems so secure, the termination of misery so certain; *yet something*

> "Makes us rather bear the ills we have,
> Than fly to others which we know not of."

BOADICEA MOURNING THE LOSS OF HER CHILD.

Chapter XXVII.

JOURNAL OF BOADICEA.—PART XXV.

Burial of Little Hubert.

{79} With my own hands, beside his father's resting-place, in a valley between two mountains, I dug my little Hubert's grave. I laid him in it, uttered over him all the prayers I could remember, for my racked brain was too much tortured for memory to do its perfect work; and then I planted his little grave with flowers.

This done, I fell upon the grave. Mrs. Munroe has since told me, that I must have remained there in a sort of trance for a number of hours, for, as I had insisted upon fulfilling my heavy and fearful task alone, she had not accompanied me, and thinking every hour would bring me home, she did not seek for me till sunset.

I have a glimmering recollection of going home with her, of the lonely house, of gathering my baby's toys and clothes together, and then I remember weeping very much, and after that all is a black, dark blank again. {80}

I again fell ill, this time so seriously, that Mrs. Munroe despaired of ever seeing me rise from my bed.

When I again was able to stand upon my feet, I could scarcely totter along, so weakened had I become. Well, well,—"Whom the Lord loveth, he chasteneth."[1]

---

1. Hebrews 12:6 (KJV).

CHAPTER XXVIII

JOURNAL OF BOADICEA.—PART XXVI.

Jeannette Boisrouge is Pursued—Flies to Boadicea—Description of
Jeannette—Her Previous Sufferings.

AND now let me speak of the sufferings of another. Among the
young persons belonging to the colony, but like myself, *in* not *of*
it, was a young girl, named Jeannette Boisrouge, a French girl, with
strong religious principles, and a good education for a person oc-
cupying the standing in society to which she belonged.

Being pursued by the importunities of Holmes, and knowing
from Mrs. Munroe, that I had been made to suffer therefrom, and
actuated by fear at the revelation of Mrs. Munroe, that Holmes
had been one of my husband's murderers, she fled to me from her
father's house.

I will here describe Jeannette. She was the prettiest French girl
I ever remember to have seen. She was a native of Normandy, and
had all the healthy beauty of the natives of that country. Her features were not particularly regular; her nose was decidedly retrousse;
but nevertheless, piquant and charming; her eyes large, black as
sloes, and her hair a rich glossy chesnut brown; her cheeks were
ruddy with beautiful health, and her form plump, and at the same
time that it was rather too short, was not wanting in that indescribable tournure which distinguishes the French girl, even in low life.

My readers may have seen a little picture representing "Rigolette,"
in Sue's "Mysteres de Paris."[1] She is depicted looking up from her
work at her canary bird, and has the three-cornered handkerchief
upon her head, which the fashion has now designated by her name.
Jeannette Boisrouge was the fac-simile of this sketch. Hers was the
same arch, yet modest and composed countenance.

When she entered my room, the poor girl's feelings overcame
her; she had, since the death of my boy, frequently visited me, and
we had become much attached to each other. She was much surprised to find me so feeble and emaciated.

---

1. *Les Mystères de Paris,* by Joseph Marie Eugène Sue (1804–1857), was
one of the first French novels to appear originally in serial form. It was
published in 1842 and 1843 in the French periodical, *Journal des débats.*

JEANNETTE BOISROUGE.

"Ah, Madame Boadicie!" exclaimed she, "what have been my sufferings, mais extreme, vraiment c'est trop fort pour moi!²" and she sank back in her chair, and the tears streamed down her face.

According to her statement, her father, old Boisrouge, as veritable a rascal as ever lived, was one of the confederates of Holmes, and {81} had persecuted her for some time, in order to induce her to become the scoundrel's *spiritual* wife.

Jeannette strenuously refused. She was, however, no match for Holmes and her father's villainous plotting and determination. First, in order to coerce her to their wishes, her father had, at the instigation of Holmes, deprived her of her best clothes, and of every little luxury which their circumstances admitted of their using.

Secondly, in order to "make her open her eyes to the excellencies of ce bon Monsieur Holmes," and to conclude the bargain (Holmes

---

2 "Really this is too much for me!"

having agreed to pay her father a certain sum for her person), Boisrouge had severely beaten her.

Her admirer and betrothed, Aldolphe Bertrand, a well-looking young French *garçon*, had been spirited mysteriously away. It was stated that the Indians had killed him, but one of the peccadilloes of the Mormons consists in disguising themselves in Indian costume, and waylaying such persons as are obnoxious to them, and putting them {82} to death, after first appropriating such moneys as they might have about them. Numbers were known to have disappeared in this manner: the blame then fell upon the Indians, whom such of the colony as were deceived into believing them the true malefactors, became more than ever anxious to exterminate. Even those poor savages were incapable of committing deeds so infamous, so bloodthirsty, and so cruel, as were common practices of the Mormon Elders, under the name of religion.[3]

The father of Jeannette was one of those persons on whose face nature seemed to have written *"villain."* His bad, small, twinkling eyes; his sallow and mottled skin; his sensual and cunning mouth; his small squat figure, more like that of a low Dutch boor, than of a native of France; each and all of these characteristics seemed to mark him out as not only the greatest rascal, but the ugliest rascal also, upon the settlement.

I could easily credit Jeannette's assertions, and fervently pity her tears, for no one who saw old Boisrouge would hesitate to believe him capable of any or every cruelty and vicious act.

---

3. This passage seems prophetic, as it was published two years before the Mountain Meadows Massacre, in which Mormons disguised themselves as Indians in order to kill settlers passing through Southern Utah. In fact, accusations of Mormons dressing as Indians to kill travelers were made as early as 1850 by William Smith, the brother of the Prophet Joseph Smith, who was excommunicated from the Church by Brigham Young in 1845. See W. Paul Reeve, *Religion of a Different Color: Race and the Mormon Struggle for Whiteness* (New York: Oxford University Press, 2014), 90–91.

CHAPTER XXIX.

JOURNAL OF BOADICEA.—PART XXVII.

Jeannette is gagged and carried away.

WE were a long time in earnest conversation, and many were the horrors which Jeannette revealed to me as having fallen under her observation, since she had become a resident among the Mormons.

Murders, seductions, thefts, all manner of iniquity was so customary that all were becoming alike hardened and callous. The general voice was hushed in consternation. Some, even among the Mormons, who like my poor Hubert, had been led to believe in the inspiration and piety of the elders, were horrified at the extent of crime perpetrated; but at each revolt, the rebellious party was sure to disappear from all eyes.

It is unnecessary for me to state here all the horrors with relation to the Mormons, which I know to be *facts*, both from my own knowledge, and the information abundantly and recklessly afforded to all who feel disposed to inquire into this subject, which should be a matter of vital interest to all, for who, among the happiest and most peaceful families of the United States, can feel assured that the inspiration of the devil will not lead some member of those happy circles to depart, and (under *demoniac possession*, for such I deem the Mormon influence) to blaspheme, and commit such vices and crimes as I have already exposed to the reader? {83}

I still continued in conversation with Jeannette Boisrouge, when Holmes, accompanied by the same masked individual as had accompanied Howard (I recognized his gaunt and stooping figure), entered the room where we sat. I have since learned that Cephysia Brown informed him that Jeannette Boisrouge was seeking shelter with me.

Holmes approached Jeannette, and in a rough manner desired her to go with him, saying that he would "show her the way back to her father." She replied, that she preferred remaining where she was.

"Mademoiselle Boisrouge is visiting me," interposed I, "and I am by no means tired of her company."—Though outwardly calm, I was really trembling in every limb.

JEANNETTE IS GAGGED AND CARRIED AWAY.

"Her father has promised me that she should not leave his mansion, except as my wife, and I will bring her to terms, if he can't," answered Holmes rudely.

"If you wish me to become your *maitresse*—what you call wife," said Jeannette in her broken English—"You take one very strange way to pay your court. I think you are one very much bad, wicked man, and I never will become your *maitresse*—your mistress—monsieur; nevare—nevare. All that *une pauvre fille comme moi*— {84} a poor girl like me—has to boast is her *vertue, sa discretion, et moi je suis discrete, oui, monsieur, la discretion meme.*"

"You may as well hush that gibberish and come with me; for Madame Boadicea here can tell you that if fair means don't serve, I'll try foul.

"I am not a man to be baffled by *any* woman," continued he, as he received no answer from Jeannette, whose eye I in vain endeavored to catch, in order to give her a look of warning.

"Cannot you allow Jeannette to remain here until morning, at least," said I, "and in the mean time apprise her father that she is visiting me? He is her proper escort about the country, not yourself."

I hoped by this means to gain time either to conceal Jeannette in my house or at Mrs. Munroe's, and thus, if possible, baffle Holmes and old Boisrouge.

"No; she *shall* go with me," answered Holmes; "I have been trifled with quite long enough." With this he approached her, and placed his hand roughly upon her shoulder. He then rapidly exchanged a look of intelligence and instruction with his athletic companion. In an instant this colossal man had gagged Jeannette, enveloped her in a cloak, and laid her in a vehicle which stood outside the door—it being a sort of covered wagon. The isolation of my abode afforded singular facilities for such acts as this being lawlessly perpetrated, without attracting the notice of the neighbors. Holmes then mounted into the wagon, and the tall individual drove it away.

I remained behind, trembling and perplexed, yet still determined to rouse the indignation of the neighbors against Boisrouge and Holmes, and, if possible, lead to the liberation of poor Jeannette from the hands of the latter.

CHAPTER XXX.

JOURNAL OF BOADICEA.—PART XXVIII.

Attempt to carry off Boadicea—Her Imprisonment.

ONE evening, while I was deliberating in what manner to achieve this purpose, Howard, from whose pursuit I had imagined myself to be at last delivered, entered the garden-gate, and presently the room where I was sitting. He approached me with his usual smirk. I felt every nerve within me thrill with horror, hatred and fear at the sight of one of the murderers of my beloved husband.

Howard seated himself. My heart palpitated with fear under his detestable influence; and fluttered in my breast like a poor charmed bird under the serpent's fascinating eye. In a few moments, and {85} after looking in a strange manner at me, he began the conversation thus:

"Has time wrought no change in the feelings of dislike you formerly entertained towards me?"

"Yes," said I; "I detest you a thousand times more heartily; and it fills me now with double horror and repugnance that I see in you the assassin, the vile murderer of an innocent man—whom you have made way with, in order, as you hope, the more easily to seduce his widowed wife."

"You assert what you do not know to be true. Did you see me kill your husband? Do you pretend to assert that?"

"I saw you gazing with exultation upon his breathless corpse," answered I; "and at the last judgment, you know well, it is you who will be called upon to answer for his murder."

"I deny that," answered Howard—(no Mormon scruples or hesitates an instant to utter the most preposterous and barefaced lie, or to assert that black is white and white black)—"I deny that; and even had I done so, it were no murder. He had deserted us—was about to fly; and it is allowable to execute summary justice upon all apostates to our holy creed."

"Do not thus blaspheme," answered I.

"But this is not my errand. Like Banquo, Hubert is 'buried; he cannot come out of his grave;'[1] and I have come here to reason with

---

1. From *Macbeth*, Act V, scene 1, line 43: "Banquo's buried; he cannot come out on 's grave." As they are here, the words are spoken by the person responsible for Banquo's murder, Lady Macbeth.

[NO CAPTION]

you. Why will you be so mad as to refuse the position I offer you? As my favorite wife, you will have nothing to do—live in luxury, attended upon by my ardent and vigilant love—the object of envy to many, and at the same time be fitting your soul for that salvation which alone can come to such as fulfil the will of the Lord, as revealed through his prophet, the sainted Joseph Smith."

I made no answer. I sat inwardly quaking with fear, and praying that the earth might open and swallow me into its very depths. No such providential escape, however, was afforded me. As well might I have been in the power of the great enemy of fallen man.

I cannot give a very clear account of what followed. I merely am able to state that, after more preamble, Howard finally offered to marry me, and leave the settlement. Even had I formed any attachment for this wicked man, I should have been certain of the insincerity of this proposition: for the manner by which he had obtained is first wife from the States was by seducing her from her parents' roof, and by effecting a sham marriage. I am merely able to state that I was then seized—I presume by Howard and another person waiting to assist him, but till then unseen—I was gagged, as Jeannette had been, and blindfolded, and then I was sensible of being lifted into some vehicle, which started off, while I remained in it, in a sitting posture, but in total darkness, pinioned and gagged.

At last, after a long time, during which it seemed to me that the wagon made a circuit, I was lifted therefrom in the arms of some {86} man and carried up a flight of stairs—then across a gallery. Then it appeared to me that a room was entered by my bearer. In a few moments I found myself free, able to see, and seated alone in a large and splendidly furnished room, hung with paintings and large mirrors, in which were also sofas and every thing appertaining to the toilet. A large curtain, hung across the lower part of the room, seemed to divide it from another chamber. All was silent, and I utterly alone.

[NO CAPTION]

CHAPTER XXXI.

JOURNAL OF BOADICEA.—PART XXIX.

Boadicea's Self-defence—Finds Cosmetics—The bloody Farce—The
Escape—Finds Cave—Cephysia's Remorse.

{87} PRESENTLY Howard entered the room. "Here, madam, you
will abide until such time as you may choose to consider me your
husband."

"That will never be," answered I, "if I stay here forever."

"Oh! very well, very well. In the mean time I am determined
to taste the sweetness of those delicate lips." With these words the
wretch approached me.

I had improved the few moments of solitude by looking round
the room, to find some instrument or weapon with which to defend myself, in case Howard attempted to pollute my person by his
touch. I would rather have died, than voluntarily have even shaken
hands with the murderer of my poor Hubert.

In a drawer of the toilet-table I discovered, among other cosmetics, a bottle of rouge, the qualities of which fluid were extolled on

CEPHYSIA BECOMES INSANE.

a label outside of the vial, and pasted fast to it. I know not why I placed it in my bosom.

As Howard approached me, I exclaimed, "You shall be baffled, fiend that you are! Sooner will I die than suffer your lips to approach mine!" Then I made a gesture as if stabbing myself, which broke the fragile vial in my bosom, and covered the front of my dress with the fluid rougeheavily, as if dead. The whole deception was favored by the gloom of the apartment.

"Great heavens!" exclaimed Howard, "she has killed herself!" He then approached me, and after gazing at me a moment, while I assumed the fixed features of a corpse, he rushed out of the room.

I rose instantly to my feet, ran to the curtain. I there found the iron grating of a balcony opening upon a flight of steps which led to the ground. By this entrance Howard had entered the apartment, but had left it by a large door on the left.

I soon reached the ground, and running along close to it, like a lapwing, I found that I was in a lonely spot; at a little distance from me rose a mountain. I bent my steps in the direction of this moun-

[NO CAPTION]

tain, with the intention of hiding myself in some of the woods; if danger threatened, I had determined to mount some tree.

After walking a long while, palpitating with fear and fatigue, I arrived at a cave, wherein I entered. In the calm moonlight which bathed the spot, I surveyed myself. My dress appeared saturated with blood. I now occupied myself with removing the broken glass, which had cut me severely. {89}

After a few moments, I noticed that a shadow was flung across the mouth of the cave, and therefore hastily withdrew to its dark depths. A tall form, (clad in male attire,) which I then supposed to be that of a young man, now entered at the mouth of the cave.

The new-comer now assumed a seat at the left side, and panting with fatigue, thus remained for a few moments. Then a deep sigh seemed to rive the stranger's breast, and a sort of wailing lamentation now commenced in a wild voice, which I immediately recognized as feminine, and that of Cephysia.

"Oh, fate! fate!" exclaimed the poor maniac, "how the fiends pursue me! There! there!" exclaimed she, wildly starting; "there is

Hubert's pale ghost. How sad he looks! No, no!" continued she, assuming the voice of humble entreaty, "do not, do not ask me for the child!"

Imagine what I felt. Alone at night, all still, far from human habitation, in a dark cave with my direst foe, my fiercest enemy, and that enemy a maniac!

Shuddering, my very teeth chattering with irrepressible fear, I remained crouched in the depths of the cave, while the maniac still continued her wild ravings.

CHAPTER XXXII.

JOURNAL OF BOADICEA.—PART XXX.

Suicide of Cephysia—Boadicea Assumes Cephysia's Clothing.

{90} SUDDENLY the moon was vailed in dark clouds; Cephysia now arose—her tall form seemed to become of gigantic height in the pervading gloom. The clouds broke away.

"Nay! come again!" she exclaimed wildly, "come once more! Ere I depart I will tell thee all, thou avenging spirit." Then, as if revealing a fearful secret, and appearing to approach the invisible subject of her ravings,

"I have killed him," said she, "I have killed him! Nay! do not shake your head thus sadly! Is it not better that one more of this doomed world's poor creatures is laid with the quiet dead! the quiet dead! the quiet dead!" repeated she. The last words seemed to please her.

Then folding her hands across her breast, and as if her mortal agony was seated there, she uttered deep and fearful groans.

"All doomed—all doomed! Fire will fall—the sword will slay—disease will exterminate!—all, all are doomed; and when the fair earth no longer holds one living thing, then, perhaps, the foul fiend will be lulled to rest."

"'The fire is never quenched,' 'the worm dieth not,'[1]" she recommenced; "the worm devoureth, and it dieth not! it dieth not! Would that death would come to me! I am worn out—I am weary—I know not rest." With these words she sank upon the earth.

"There, there! it comes—it will speak to me again!" cried the mad woman, again rising to her feet.

"No, no! I cannot bear it! I cannot bear it! Death! death! death! Peace! Rest! rest! Death! death!"

With these words she ran from the cave. I followed stealthily. Presently the maniac reappeared; she loosened the cravat from her neck, which formed a part of her male attire; then she unbound her black hair, and divested herself of the frock-coat she wore; she then uncoiled a rope, which she fastened about her neck, and set off at a run.

---

1. The phrase, "Where their worm dieth not, and the fire is not quenched," is used multiple times to describe hell in the ninth chapter of Mark.

I followed her, but when I at last succeeded in reaching her, I found the unfortunate creature—whose swift run enabled her to get the advance of me—had hung herself upon a tree which grew by the wayside.

With trembling hands I unfastened the still swinging body, and at last, after much trouble, the darkness which the pervading clouds caused ever and anon impeding my movements, I succeeded in loosen- {91} ing the rope, which was now deeply imbedded in the skin of the poor woman's throat. Life was totally extinct. A sudden thought now struck me—to possess myself of Cephysia's attire, and therein, if possible, to escape!

I speedily divested her form of the clothing she wore, and garbed myself in it. It was a fearful task! This done, I clothed the corpse in my own dress.

I then laid Cephysia's body upon the ground, closed the staring eyes, crossed the hands upon her bosom, and uttering with still trembling lips the prayer for the dead, I left the dead body to its eternal rest.

CHAPTER XXXIII.

JOURNAL OF BOADICEA.—PART XXXI.

Hears of the Murder of Jeannette Boisrouge—Recognizes Holmes
and Boisrouge.

I PURSUED my way, looking out for some shelter, in which, if possible, to lie down, and forget in sleep the terrible drama of the night. Far ahead of me, I saw a sort of wooden scaffold, and near it several benches. It appeared to have been erected for some religious ceremony. Several trees stood near, in a clump together.

I now heard voices in the distance. Hurrying on, I succeeded in reaching the clump of trees. Mounting with rapidity, (I found that my male attire facilitated rapidity of motion,) I ascended one of the trees and concealed myself among the branches. I now recognized the faces of Boisrouge and of Holmes; they were in conversation.

"It was no fault of mine," said Holmes, with whom Boisrouge seemed to be quarreling; "if she had minded what I said to her, I should not have done it. I did not mean to kill her—she scratched and struck me, and acted like a tigress, the moment I untied her hands, and then I told her to desist, but she would not. I forgot the whip-handle had a leaden top, when I struck, but down she dropped in a minute, as if she had been shot, and just as dead as a door nail. But it was no fault of mine that she chose to show fight—I'll be damned if it was!"

"But then you've cheated me," answered old Boisrouge; "it ish not so much la fille, ze girl hercef; it is mine monish, mine monish, vat you did promish me for her, if I did try for make her be your vife; vat you did promish me, entends tu, scélérat!"

"None of that eternal gibberish," answered Holmes. "I don't like it, and I won't stand it,—no, I won't. She's dead, and I'm sorry for it; but a bargain's a bargain. I bargained for a live girl, and not a dead girl, Boisrouge! so none of your nonsense, or I might take it {93} into my head to finish you too, you know; so don't be troublesome!" Here Boisrouge left Holmes, muttering something about being re-venged. Holmes stretched himself out on one of the benches beneath the trees, and went to sleep. I felt myself turn deathly faint at thus suddenly hearing of the "murder most foul" of poor Jeannette.

OLD BOISROUGE AND HOLMES.

I scarcely know how I managed to keep my seat in the tree, so much overcome was I; but fear, and the presence of great danger, will do much to strengthen the nerves even of a woman. It is difficult for me to make this narrative more in the manner of a novel, and therefore, more interesting to the reader.

Actual events as they occur, seldom happen in the order laid down by romancers and poets. The *vraisemble* and the *vraie* are very different.[1] I relate events as they happen, and add to the web of realities no embroidery suited to fiction.

Such events as I here lay before the reader, are *daily* occurrences among the Mormons. No better idea of pandemonium can be conceived; it is a veritable hell upon God's fair and beautiful earth. The blood of the murdered, the crushed hearts of the despairing cry out for vengeance!

The car of Juggernaut is not more fearful in its slaughter than the fell influence of the Mormon faith. Nay! it is far worse, for that slays the body merely beneath its crushing wheels: this destroys the purity of the immortal soul.

---

1. The French terms *vraisemble* and *vraie* translate roughly as "that which is credible" and "that which is true."

CHAPTER XXXIV.

JOURNAL OF BOADICEA.—PART XXXII.

Holmes' house is Fired—Holmes and Howard are killed by the fall of a Rafter.

While Holmes still slept beneath the tree, I surveyed the surface of the country, and discovered that I was not far form the residence of Holmes himself, a mansion painted yellow, with dark shutters.

I now observed a lurid light arise from the roof of the house. It increased, smoke rose up in volumes, with streaks of flame and large sparks. Presently I heard the screams of women. Then male voices gave the cry of "Fire! fire!"

This awoke Holmes, who started up, rubbed his eyes, and looked in the direction of the fire light.

"My house on fire!" exclaimed he. "Sure enough!" and off he started at a run.

At this moment a horseman rode up: it was Howard. He stopped Holmes, and related to him my supposed suicide; but stated that when he had returned to the apartment, he found that {94} some one had "effected an entrance and carried the body away." He stated that he was then going to Mrs. Munroe's, where he supposed he should find my corpse. Holmes, who continually interrupted him with attempts to assert the matter of his house being on fire, now succeeded in persuading him to go with him to assist in extinguishing the flames. They accordingly rode off, Holmes having mounted behind Howard on his brown horse. I know not what induced me to follow. Perhaps it was a vague presentiment that the villains were going to their doom.

Arrived at the fire, each exerted himself to the utmost to extinguish the flames; but they gained headway with great rapidity. A woman, in a loose white dress, now appeared at one of the windows. She held a child in her arms, and shrieked for help. I recognized one of the wives of Bernard Yale, and recollected the marriage between Holmes and herself, which had taken place within a year.

Holmes and Howard now mounted together upon a ladder, and entered the window where she stood. The flames now burst forth below them. Howard took the woman in his arms, and Holmes seized the child. The flames from below now spouted up through the window beneath that where the group stood. They caught the ladder. In a moment the lower part was burned to a char, and it fell. At this moment, and while Holmes and Howard were seeking the ladder by which to descend, the flames burst through the floor of the room wherein they stood. They saw their fate, and one unearthly yell broke from both. The fall of a rafter struck both down, as well as the woman and child. The roof now fell in with a loud crash, and amid the shrieks of the bystanders, consisting of the other wives of Holmes and his numerous family of children. Thus, in one night, did death fall upon my three vindictive enemies and remorseless pursuers. In spite of my horror and dismay, I drew a long breath— "the sigh of a great deliverance."

I now started to return to the shelter of the scaffolding, until at least the daybreak should enable me the better to see where I was. This spot gained, I lay down upon one of the benches, and fell into a heavy and unrefreshing sleep, broken by dreams of the most horrible description. Again did I imagine myself in the house of Howard; again did I behold the suicide of Cephysia; and again did I see the falling rafters crush Holmes, Howard, the woman and her child! At last I awoke—and I was glad to awake—for I had no real rest; and the horrors of such dreams almost equalled those of the realities they revived.

I stood up—and having fairly aroused myself, I saw it was dawn. I now gathered my long hair in a knot, and concealed it beneath the straw hat which formed a part of my dress. I bathed my face in a brook which ran beneath the trees; and, making a staff of a limb of one of the trees, I began to walk on. {95}

CHAPTER XXXV.

JOURNAL OF BOADICEA.—PART XXIII.

Boadicea meets a Party—Hides Herself—Overhears Conversation—
Recognizes Friends—Joins them.

I now saw a party, consisting of a tall woman, an old man, and a young lad and girl, approaching me. I concealed myself behind one of the bushes, which break the monotony of the country, and crouched down. I did this partly because I was still too unaccustomed to my male dress not to feel ashamed to be seen in it by persons of the sex to which it more properly appertained, and partly to discover whether those who approached were likely to prove friends or enemies. The old man, whose countenance wore a look of deep sadness, now spoke:

"Would to Heaven," said he, "that we could again reach the States! and yet how little do I dare to hope it!"

"Dear father," said the tall young woman, "we are fortunate in evading suspicion thus far. Cheer up: let us hope and persevere."

It struck me that this person spoke in a very masculine voice. On observing her closely through the branches of the bush behind which I was crouched, I saw that the lips from whence these words proceeded were marked with the faint down which announces an incipient moustache; and, in spite of a close cap, the face had the bold, bright look of a boy.

Presently the old man—as I had supposed the first speaker to be—disengaged his long white beard from his jaws—thus discovering the thick, short, black beard of a young man. Another movement removed a white wig; and I then recognized Robert Hoffman, a young German musician, who had arrived some seven or eight months before, and with whose sister, the young girl before mentioned, I had some acquaintance.

The young lad now began relating the circumstances of the fire, and I took courage to reveal myself. A long conversation followed. I found that my friends had arranged, by secret correspondence with some relations in the States, and through the means of bribed Indians, to meet them half way between the States and the Mormon settlement, armed and provided with water and provision. They kindly invited me to join them; which I did not, as it may be supposed, hesitate to do.

BOADICEA'S PARTY STARTS FOR THE STATES.

CHAPTER XXXVI.

JOURNAL OF BOADICEA.—PART XXIV, AND LAST.

{97} I WILL not here describe the long and weary journey home. Our friends met us, as had been agreed. The tedious route and monotonous journey has been too often detailed.

After the journey, we arrived safely at the States; and although my health suffered severely during my residence among the Mormons and the return home, I am now partially recovered.

I now bid farewell to my readers—trusting that they have not found my story tedious, and that the time may soon come when such horrors as it details may be among the things which

> "Have been, and are not."[1]

FAREWELL!

THE END.

---

1. "And the good delight to hear of the past evils of such as are now freed from them, not because they are evils, but because they have been and are not." From Book Ten of Augustine's *Confessions*.

APPENDIX 1.

Extracted from: Henry Mayhew, *The Mormons, or, Latter-day Saints: A Contemporary History*, London, 1852, 304–12.

{304} According to Mr. Bowes, the author of the pamphlet from which we have already quoted, the social life of the Mormons is an extensive and well organized system of licentiousness. Joseph Smith, he tells us, taught a system of polygamy; that he sought to seduce Nancy Rigdon, Sarah M. Pratt, and others; that, in some instances, he was repulsed, in others, he succeeded. Joseph Smith is also accused of having endeavoured to secure Martha H. Brotherton, once of Manchester, for his friend Brigham Young; in both cases attempting to influence his victims by persuading them that he had received a revelation from God, justifying adultery, seduction, and other sins. A letter from Martha Brotherton sets forth the whole charge against Joseph Smith and Brigham Young, and if to be believed, proves it:—

"I had been at Nauvoo near three weeks, during which time my father's family received frequent visits from Elders Brigham Young and Heber C. Kimball, two of the Mormon Apostles; when, early one morning, they both came to my brother-in-law's (John M'Ilwrick's) house, at which place I then was on a visit, and particularly requested me to go and spend a few days with them. I told them I could not at that time, as my brother-in-law was not at home; however, they urged me to go the next day, and spend one day with them. The day being fine, I accordingly went. * * * * He led me up some stairs to a small room, the door of which was locked, and on it the following inscription; 'Positively no admittance.' He observed, 'Ah! brother Joseph must be sick, for, strange to say, he is not here. Come down into the tithing-office, Martha.' He then left me in the tithing-office, and went out, I know not where. In this office were two men writing, one of whom, William Clayton, I had seen in England; the other I did not know. Young came in, and seated himself before me, and asked where Kimball was. I said he had gone out. He said it was all right. Soon after, Joseph came in, and spoke to one of the clerks, and then went up stairs, followed by Young. Immediately after, Kimball came in. 'Now, Martha,' said he, 'the Prophet has come; come up stairs.' I went, and we found Young and the Prophet alone. I was introduced to the Prophet by Young. Joseph offered me his seat; and, to my astonishment, the moment I was seated, Joseph and Kimball walked out of the room, and left me with Young, who arose, locked the door, closed the window, and drew the curtain. He then came and sat before me, and said, 'This is our private room, Martha.' 'Indeed, sir,' said I, 'I must be highly honoured to be permitted to enter it.' He smiled, and then proceeded—'Sister Martha, I want to ask you a few questions; will you answer them?' 'Yes, Sir,' said I. * * * * 'To come to the point more closely,' said he, 'have not you an affection for {305} me, that, were it lawful and right, you could accept of me for your husband and companion?' * * * * * I therefore said, 'If it was lawful and right, perhaps I might; but you know, sir, it is not.' 'Well, but,' said he, 'brother Joseph has had a revelation from God that it is lawful and right for a man to have two wives; for, as it was in the days of Abraham, so it shall be in these last days, and whoever is the first that is willing to take up the cross will receive the greatest blessings; and if you will accept of me, I will take you straight to the celestial kingdom; and if you will have me in this world, I will have you in that which is to come, and brother Joseph will marry us here to-day, and you can go home this evening, and your parents will not know anything about it.' 'Sir,' said I, 'I should not like to do anything of the kind without the permission of my parents.' * * * * 'Well,' said he, 'I will have a kiss, any how,' and then rose, and said he would bring Joseph. He then unlocked the door, and took the key, and locked me up alone. He was absent about ten minutes, and then returned with Joseph. 'Well,' said Young, 'sister Martha would be willing if she knew it was lawful and right before God.' 'Well, Martha,' said Joseph, 'it is lawful and right before God—I *know* it is. Look here, sis.; don't you believe in me?' I did not answer. 'Well, Martha,' said Joseph, 'just go a-head, and do as Brigham wants you to—he is the best man in the world, except me.' 'O!' said Brigham, 'then you are as good.' 'Yes,' said Joseph. 'Well,' said Young, 'we believe Joseph to be a Prophet. I have known him near eight years, and always found him the same.' 'Yes,' said Joseph, 'and I know that this is lawful and right before God, and if there is any sin in it, I will answer for it before God; and I have the keys of the kingdom, and whatever I bind on earth is bound in heaven, and whatever I loose on earth is loosed in heaven; and if you will accept of Brigham, you shall be blessed—God shall bless you, and my blessing shall rest upon you; and if you will be led by him you will do well; for I know Brigham will take care of you; and if he don't do his duty to you, come to me and I will make him; and if you do not like it in a month or two, come to me, and I will make you free again; and if he turns you off, I will take you on."'

Another deposition, sworn by Melissa Schindle, describes similar practices. Mr. Bowes also describes certain hidden orgies practised in the Nauvoo Temple, which are sufficiently suspicious. The statement is sworn to by J.M. Gee Van Dusen and Maria Van Dusen, who profess to have been initiated into the mysteries. The seventh degree in the Temple relates to "the Spiritual Wife Doctrine." {306} "Those who have attained to this are taught," say these witnesses, "that they are no more under obligations to their husband, if they have one, and it is their privilege to leave their lawful husband, and take another;" and, "it is the privilege of some kings to have scores, yes, hundreds of queens, especially the King of kings, Brigham Young, the present Mormon god in California,—(or devil, I should say, for I have reason to believe he is the wickedest man now on the face of the earth;) and, further, as we are all made kings and queens by this secret farce, the foundation for a kingdom is laid also. And here is the secret of the Spiritual Wife Doctrine:—Their kingdom is to consist in their own posterity, and the more wives the greater opportunity of getting a large kingdom, of course; so it is an object to one who holds this doctrine sacred, as thousands do, to get all the women he can, consequently it subjects that portion of the female sex which he has influence over eventually to literal ruin."

This reason, which may hold good for polygamy, obviously does not for adultery or fornication, into one or both of which the Spiritual Wife practice resolves itself. There is in such an erroneous argument, ground for suspicion of prejudice in relation to the statement adduced as its basis. And as the Mormon authorities positively deny that Joseph Smith was guilty of the charge often alleged in justificating his murder, it is a motive of caution in the receipt of evidence. We must remember, too, that Smith universally, in all his letters, revelations, and speeches, denounced adultery and fornication. Subject as all founders of religious systems are to calumny, we cannot resist the doubt that there may have been mis-representation and exaggeration, both as to the character of Joseph Smith and the cause of his untimely end. At any rate, and under any circumstances, it is impossible to justify the acts of his enemies, either in the persecution of his followers, or in the circumstances of his death. The fanaticism that destroyed him is to be condemned quite as strongly as his own.

It is further stated, that the Mormon candidate for holy orders, among other promises, makes oath, that he "will never touch a daughter of Adam, unless she be given him of the Lord,"—thus consecrating licentiousness with the holiest sanctions. But it must be remarked that these charges are given under cover of "secret rev-elations of the church—none but the faithful being permitted to have the privilege" of prostituting the daughters and wives of their friends and acquaintances. It is affirmed, on this covert evidence, that the Mormons "teach that this system is what we are to under-stand by the blessings of Abraham, Isaac, and Jacob." We are further told, that there is an institution of "Cloistered Saints," {307} which forms the "highest order of the Mormon harem, and is composed of women, whether married or unmarried, as *secret* spiritual wives." This is Mr. Bowes's statement; who likewise requires us to believe that "When an apostle, high priest, elder, or scribe, conceives an affection for a female, and has ascertained her views on the subject, he communicates confidentially to the prophet his love affair, and requests him to inquire of the Lord whether or not it would be right and proper for him to take unto himself this woman for his spiritual wife. It is no obstacle whatever to this spiritual marriage if one or both of the parties should happen to have a husband or wife already united to them according to the laws of the land."

"The prophet," continues Mr. Bowes, "puts this singular question to the Lord, and, if he receives an answer in the affirmative, which is always the case where the parties are in favour with the president, the parties assemble in the lodge-room, accompanied by a duly autho-rized administrator, and place themselves, kneeling, before the altar; the administrator commences the ceremony by saying:—

"'You, separately and jointly, in the name of Jesus Christ, the son of God, do solemnly covenant and agree that you will not disclose any matter relating to the sacred act now in progress of consummation, whereby any Gentile shall come to a knowledge of the secret purposes of this order, or whereby the saints may suffer persecution, your lives being the forfeit.'"

After the vow of assent is given by each of the pair, the administrator proceeds to pronounce them "*one flesh*, in the name of the Father, and of the Son, and of the Holy Ghost."

"The parties," it is said, by the same authority, "leave the cloister with generally a firm belief, at least on the part of the female, in the sacredness and validity of the ceremonial, and consider themselves as united in spiritual marriage, the duties and privileges of which are in no particular different from those of any other marriage covenant."

Among the stray statements quoted on more or less evidence touching this subject, we find that William Arrowsmith, before mentioned, "talked to Joseph Smith about Martha Brotherton's case. Smith did not deny what Martha relates, but stated that Brigham Young and he did it to try her, as they had heard an evil report of her." We are told, also, upon the same sort of authority, that "Whelock," another Mormon leader, married three wives, the first Parrish, the second Rose. Grand jury took him up for bigamy. He married a decent girl at Birmingham, and she would have to live with the American wives educated in bad families.

Accusations like these naturally lead us to look into the recognised {308} documents of the Mormons themselves for corroboration and support. We turn, accordingly, to "The Book of Doctrines and Covenants," for such articles of law and regulation as may relate to these alleged practices. These revelations, it should be observed, notwithstanding the limitation in the title page, are not all given to Joseph Smith, but are extended to divers of his apostles likewise. In one purporting to be received by Martin Harris, the opulent Mormon already spoken of as one of the witnesses, and who is warned in it "not to covet" his "own property, but impart it freely to the printing of the Book of Mormon," we find this admonition published—"And again I command thee, that thou shalt not covet thy neighbour's wife, nor seek thy neighbour's life." Not less explicit is the revelation vouchsafed to Joseph Smith himself.

"And again, I say, thou shalt not kill; but he that killeth shall die. Thou shalt not steal; and he that stealeth and will not repent, shall be cast out. Thou shalt not lie; he that lieth and will not repent, shall be cast out. Thou shalt love thy wife with all thy heart, and shalt cleave unto her and none else; and he that looketh upon a woman to lust after her, shall deny the faith, and shall not have the Spirit, and if he repents not, he shall be cast out. Thou shalt not commit adultery; and he that committeth adultery and repenteth not shall be cast out; but he that has committed adultery and repents with all his heart, and forsaketh it, and doeth it no more, thou shalt forgive; but if he doeth it again, he shall not be forgiven, but shall be cast out. Thou shalt not speak evil of thy neighbour, nor do him any harm. Thou knowest my laws concerning these things are given in my scriptures; he that sinneth and repenteth not, shall be cast out.

"And, verily I say unto you, as I have said before, he that looketh on a woman to lust after her, or if any shall commit adultery, in their hearts, they shall not have the Spirit, but shall deny the faith and shall fear: wherefore I, the Lord, have said that the fearful, and the unbelieving, and all liars, and whosoever loveth and maketh a lie, and the whoremonger, and the sorcerer, shall have their part in that lake which burneth with fire and brimstone which is the second death. Verily I say, that they shall not have part in the first resurrection."

Here, too, is an ordinance directing the manner of proceeding with adulterers:—

"And if any man or woman shall commit adultery, he or she shall be tried before two elders of the church or more, and every word shall be established against him or her by two witnesses of the church, and not of the enemy; but if there are more than two witnesses it is {309} better. But he or she shall be condemned by the mouth of two witnesses, and the elders shall lay the case before the church, and the church shall lift up their hands against him or her, that they may be dealt with according to the law of God. And if it can be, it is necessary that the bishop is present also. And thus ye shall do in all cases which shall come before you."

Here is another with the same purport, but including the fornicator.

"Behold, verily I say unto you, that whatever persons among you having put away their companions for the cause of fornication, or, in other words, if they shall testify before you in all lowliness of heart that this is the case, ye shall not cast them out from among you; but if ye shall find that any persons have left their companions for the sake of adultery, and they themselves are the offenders, and their companions are living, they shall be cast out from among you. And again, I say unto you, that ye shall be watchful and careful, with all inquiry, that ye receive none such among you if they are married; and if they are not married, they shall repent of all their sins, or ye shall not receive them."

Here, likewise, is an ordinance relating to marriage.

"And again, I say unto you, that whoso forbiddeth to marry is not ordained of God, for marriage is ordained of God unto man; wherefore it is lawful that he should have one wife, and they twain shall be one flesh, and all this that the earth might answer the end of its creation, and that it might be filled with the measure of man, according to his creation before the world was made."

Finally, the charge with which we are dealing is met in a direct and positive manner, as follows:—

"All legal contracts of marriage made before a person is baptised into this church should be held sacred and fulfilled. Inasmuch as this church of Christ has been reproached with the crime of fornication and polygamy; we declare that we believe that one man should have one wife; and one woman but one husband, except in case of death, when either is at liberty to marry again. It is not right to persuade a woman to be baptized contrary to the will of her husband; neither is it lawful to influence her to leave her husband. All children are bound by law to obey their parents; and to influence them to embrace any religious faith, or be baptized, or leave their parents without their consent, is unlawful and unjust. We believe that husbands, parents, and masters, who exercise control over their wives, children, and servants, and prevent them from embracing the truth, will have to answer for that sin."

Several of the epistles which are to be found scattered through {310} the publications of the sect, show that those in authority are actuated by an earnest desire to remove all cause for scandal in reference even to the most ordinary intercourse between the sexes; and if they are to be judged by their writings, we may assume that their efforts are continually directed towards the attainment of a higher morality than that commonly in vogue. For instance, in a letter to the Saints by Orson Pratt and Orson Spencer, we find the writers addressing those under their charge in the following terms:—

"The sharp edge of persecution is whetted to unwonted keenness by *lewd* men, who turn the grace of God into lasciviousness, and bring scandal and stigma upon that priesthood which is ordained to save the human family. When one member of the priesthood is polluted, however obscure, the whole body is sickened by the contagion. Speedy amputation often becomes painfully necessary. All heaven is pervaded with one common spirit of indignation. We feel as though something like fratricide, or slaying of our brethren, had been attempted: the wound is in the house of our friends. But Zion will not always mourn. Judgment is now given into her hand, and the workers of iniquity shall be cut off, and the stench of their detestable deeds will follow them; and when the seducer's and adulterer's bones are mouldering in the dust, the scent of his abominable deeds will bring upon his memory the bitter imprecations of the righteous. While the law of God has been but imperfectly appreciated, even by many of the church, these things may have been bearable through false tradition; yet, the time is now when the cloak of charity cannot, and will not, screen such offenders. Two instances of gross lewdness have occurred among the elders of this land, and we have strictly enjoined the prohibition of their re-baptism or reunion with the church, without a verbal application to the First Presidency, residing far distant in Zion. Although the spirit of seduction and lewdness has occasionally invaded the Church in its purest state, it has never obtained a particle of fellowship, neither will it do so in any future time, from any faithful servant of God. And we distinctly say to the Saints in Britain, let no artifice or cunningly devised tale ever be regarded as any apology for this gross immorality. No grade of office whatever will ever authorize any one to teach or practise this abomination. This Church is a purifier, and will refine its members as silver; and men must not think to bring into its sacred enclosure the abominations of the Gentiles, who are an adulterous and wicked generation—strange children—conceived in sin and shapen in iniquity.

"Not so with the Church of the living God. Their marriage vows are sacred, and cannot be violated with impunity; their offspring are legitimate, and not bastards conceived in sin, but holy unto the Lord; and the man or woman in this Church that contributes to illegitimacy, thereby entailing upon his or her offspring the cure of

exclusion from the congregation of the Lord, to the third generation, he or she that does it becomes detestable in the eyes of the
Lord and all good people, and their condemnation will not slum-
ber. Let none be deceived in this matter, for the eyes of the Lord will
{311} penetrate every work, and the spirit that is confirmed upon
the Saints will bear witness against all such like abominations, and
no work of iniquity will or can possibly escape detection in due
time. The nations of the earth are corrupt and abominable in these
things; but they that bear the message of the Lord must be clean:
they must keep themselves undefiled, or share in the plagues of
Babylon. Pitiable is the condition of that man who has made com-
merce of the gifts of the priesthood, like Esau. His strength is gone,
like unto Sampson's when shorn of his locks, and he becomes an
easy prey to his enemies. Who then, among the sons and daughters
of men, will lay hold upon the skirts of such fallen reprobates in
order to obtain salvation? Let those who have already spotted their
garments with these Gentile practices, prove a sufficient ensample
to deter all others. Let the beacon-light of a few examples keep others from the rocks and quicksands where scattered wrecks fearfully
remonstrate and warn!

"Dear brethren, no false delicacy shall forbid us from speaking plainly to you upon this subject. Lust, when it is conceived,
bringeth forth sin. The pure in heart have no occasion to mistake
this infallible precursor and antecedent to sin; it is easily discover-
able. It is only when the invading foe is welcomed and cherished
that sin can ever be the result. *Here* is opportunity afforded for to
consider, reflect, and *beware!* Whatever of sexual manners, dress,
or intimacy is known to cherish forbidden or ungovernable lusts,
may be a surely known to produce sin. The familiar usages of one
nation may not be equally compatible with the purity of another
people, accustomed to other usages. We do not complain of the
manners and dress of any nation, so long as they are compatible
with purity and the law of God. The salutation by kissing was practised in the Jewish nation, and it was tolerated among the members
of the primitive Church of Christ; but it was by no means a law or
necessary duty.

"The first transgression introduced the necessity of a covering,
and urged the importance of fresh laws regulating acts of decency.

Perfect purity would require no law to determine what is modest or what is perilous to virtue. The law is made for transgressors. When men can keep themselves pure in body, soul, and spirit, they then become as wise virgins, and emerge into the perfect law of boundless liberty. No person can be a successful candidate for the celestial prize that does not keep the law in all these respects. Men must learn to approximate to that state of perfect purity in which the law is written upon their hearts, so as to supersede the necessity of outward ordinances which will perish with the using.

"The pure in heart, who are fully established in the law of continency, might use the ancient salutation of a holy kiss, and other innocent familiarities of a kindred nature, with perfect impunity. But not so with all. We have need to write unto some, even as carnal and babes in Christ. Such have not already attained that steadfastness to which the Gospel calls them. What then? Is it not better that the strong bear the infirmities of the weak, and forego any practice that may cause their brother to offend?

"We therefore think it wise and expedient, and give it as our counsel ac- {312} cordingly, to the English Saints, to abstain entirely from these unbecoming familiarities through which some have been already led into gross transgression.

"If the elders wish to save their congregations, and obtain a good degree for themselves and others in the kingdom of God, let them abstain, rather, from all appearance of evil. Let those familiarities which are often the legitimate expression of innocence and the purest love, be avoided, because they may be spoken evil of by those that are without, and because the inexperienced confidence of young members is liable to be betrayed, and made a bait to folly and crime. We write unto presidents of conferences as unto wise men, to whom a hint will be sufficient, and who will readily understand what the will of the Lord is in such matters. We do not wish to multiply arbitrary laws among a people that are destined by the grace of God, and their own trustworthiness, to rise above all law into the region of ineffable light, purity, and glory. But we do, nevertheless, intend to establish laws against the invasion of the unruly and transgressors. And we wish the elders and holy women who are mothers to co-operate with us against the intrusion of Gentile abominations. And we do declare, with all sobriety in the fear of

God, and by the authority we hold from God in the holy priesthood, that a curse shall rest upon transgressors, who, with knowing
wickedness, shall hereafter violate the laws of virtue and chastity.
This is the voice of the priesthood in Zion, and the voice of God,
from the foundation of the world. Hear it, oh ye Saints throughout the British isles and adjacent countries! While God is gathering
,and will continue to gather his sons from afar, and his daughters
from the ends of the earth, he will not tolerate the obstruction of
the great and last gathering by the abominations of reprobates, that
have been cast out as refuse silver, and by their slanderous tales of
abomination, palmed upon his infant cause."

In the third General Epistle of the Presidency we find some
regulations which redound highly to the credit of the Mormon authorities. But leaving the question of the polygamy and seduction
alleged to have been, or to be still practised by the Mormons, to be
decided by the reader, upon the evidence on both sides which we
have produced, we proceed to other points.

APPENDIX 2.

Extract from: Orvilla S. Belisle, *The Prophets; or, Mormonism Unveiled*, Philadelphia: Wm. White Smith; London: Trubner & Co., 1855, 403–12.

CHAPTER XXV

THE intrigues of the prophet and his Patriarchs were only samples which the more humble followed, with such additions and emendations as they chose to adopt, and extended from the hoary sinner of four score years to the jacketed boy at school on the one side, and from the wrinkled hag bereft of every vestige of loveliness, to the miss in pantalettes, on the other. Cupid's missives flew thick, fast, and indiscriminately from the hoary head to the young miss, and from the old beldame to him who was yet unbroken by vice. From the husband and father to his neighbour's wife, or daughter, and from the wife and daughter, wherever their wanton eye rested.

The Prophet as the husband of sixty wives openly wedded, and as many sealed, was still not contented, but {404} added two more wings to his harem, in order to accommodate others he purposed to take, as his authority had become so thoroughly established that, every Mormon become so thoroughly established that, every Mormon was taxed one-tenth of all he possessed to support the priesthood,—that is—the harems of the Prophet and Patriarchs.

Approaching old age and unrestrained passions, although they bowed his form, only fed anew the unquenched fires so long indulged in, and ambition and vice now reigned supreme in his heart.

Isolated from civilization by fifteen hundred miles of wilderness, he bid defiance to all that had checked his free indulgence in ambitious schemes and debaucheries in the States.

Here, with thirty thousand subjects, he reigned supreme autocrat, holding the wealth, labour, liberty and lives of his followers at his own mercy, which was swayed by the passions that held him in bondage, and whose slave he had become. The infatuation of his subjects could not hide from them the imposition and enormities of their Leader, and the burdens cast upon the labourers to wring from them the means to support the largely stocked harems, were greater than they could bear.

To complain was to call down upon themselves heavier burdens still. They could not expect justice from the hands of the taskmaster, and they were not agreeably {405} disappointed, for equity and justice found not a step on which to rest among a people where the powerful were privileged to prey upon the weak and defenceless.

As Governor and Prophet, Young defied remonstrance and complaint, and when crushed beneath the heavy burdens enforced upon them, the poor deluded fanatics prayed for relief, he not only inflicted grievous chastisements for their temerity, but essayed to launch the thunders of eternal punishment in the world to come upon them.

Their groanings at last reached the home government, and were responded to with promises of relief—promises which were treated with defiance and contempt by the Prophet, who, in his fancied security among the fastnesses of the west, dared any attempt being made to put a stop to, or punish his crimes. Awakened at last to the necessity of fulfilling this promise,—for every civilized nation was looking on their enormity with astonishment and indignation, that a civilized people should tolerate in their territories such wanton crimes, that shamed alike humanity and the people who suffered it,—and resolved to send thither officers duly appointed and commissioned, to see that the grievances of the American citizens residing in Utah Territory were redressed, and the laws of the Union equitably administered among them.

Lemuel G. Branderbury received the appointment of {406} Chief Justice of the Supreme Court of the United States for the Territory of Utah, and Perry E. Brockus Associate Justice of the Supreme Court for the same territory with B.B. Harris as Secretary.

The Prophet-Governor received these offices with studied coldness and contempt, which, ere long broke out into open rebellion against their vested authority. His infatuated followers at once sided with their leaders, and the officers soon saw their positions were anything but enviable, as they were greeted by undisguised hostility whenever they showed themselves in the street.

The Prophet publicly denounced them and the home government, in choice billingsgate, on all occasions, even from the pulpit on the Sabbath, while they composed part of his audience; and the Patriarchs, in strict imitation of their leader, vied with each other in heaping indignities sufficient upon them to drive them from the territory, so as once more to be free to pursue their unholy depredations upon the weak and defenceless, unmolested.

"For a man to come here," said the Prophet, on one of these occasions, "and infringe upon my individual rights and privileges, and upon those of my brethren, will never meet my sanction, and I will scourge such a one until he leaves: I am after him. I informed you in my discourse that has just been read, that my religion is first and foremost with me, and I will send it to all {407} the earth, to President Pierce, whether he retains me as Governor of Utah Territory or not; and, whether I should be President of the United States, or King of Great Britain, or monarch of all the world, my religion and my God are first and foremost with me. My kingship, my presidentship, and all shall bow to that eternal priesthood which God has bestowed upon me. I have been Governor of this Territory ever since it has had one, and in all my official transactions I have acted in accordance with the priesthood. I never will infringe upon it with anything I may operate in any office; let them all go by the board, before I will be brought into a situation that will cause me to infringe upon my priesthood. In all my doings, as an Elder of Israel, as holding the keys of the priesthood to this generation, if I continue to be the governor of this territory, I shall magnify my office by my priesthood. I am and will be Governor, until God Almighty says, 'Brigham, you need not be Governor any more.' Now come on to war, whenever you think best, and we will gather out the honest until the last seed of Israel is gathered, and there is hardly enough left to elect a President, even among the Know Nothings."

As he paused in his harangue, he was greeted with shouts and clapping of hands, that assured them his sentiments were heartily concurred in by his hearers.{408}

"I have," pursued he, "ruled this people for years, and will rule them again. The Judges may remain in this territory, if they like, and draw their salaries, but they shall not try a cause, if I can prevent it." Then he continued, raising his voice to an exulting tone:—

"Zachary Taylor is dead, and gone to hell, and I am glad of it; and I prophesy in the name of Jesus Christ, by the power of the Priesthood that is upon me, that any President of the United States who lifts his finger against this people shall die an untimely death, and go to hell."

"Yes, Judge," said Heber C. Kimball, to Judge Brockus, as he laid his hand on his shoulder, "it is so, and you will know it too, for you will see him when you get there!"

With a shudder Judge Brockus turned away, as loud shouts of "Amen!" "Good!" "Hear! Hear!" greeted this sally of the Prophet, and his satellites, when the harangue was continued in a strain both blasphemous and treasonable, declaring: "He was as great a man as ever George Washington was; that if there was any more interference, there would be pulling of hair, and cutting of throats."

By this time the passions of his auditors were lashed to as great a fury as his own, and muttered threats, menacing gestures, and fierce imprecations greeted the officers, who, pale, but firm, stood silent spectators in the midst of the angry multitude. {409}

"If," said the officers, in their report of this scene, "the Prophet had but pointed his finger towards us, as an indication of a wish, we have no doubt we would have been massacred before leaving the house, for the Prophet declared afterwards that, had he but crooked his finger, 'we should have been torn in pieces.'"

The Prophet convened the Legislative body, which was composed of creatures of his own choosing, the election being irregular, and serfs from the old world, and aliens of every nation and clime, with no other naturalization than that of a Mormon baptism, being permitted to vote, and were even admitted into the Legislative body to make laws to govern free-born Americans.

The officers remonstrated, but with as little avail as all their other endeavours to carry out the laws they were sent to see executed with equity and justice to all. And still, crimes of the darkest dye went unpunished, the perpetrators shielded by the all-powerful Prophet.

This state of affairs, however, could not last long, for threatened and menaced, their steps dogged by ruffians wherever they went, the power vested in them rendered null by the inability to execute it upon thirty thousand people in open rebellion against it, they had only one thing left to them, and that was, to vacate the Territory until the Federal Government should supply the means of enforcing the laws, the Mormons set at defiance. {410}

They returned to the States and laid the disordered condition of affairs in Utah before the Government. This was a dilemma that puzzled the wisest heads, for they desired to bring the refractory Territory to terms, by force of reason, rather than coercion. One thing was certain, a Governor and Executive must be sent into the Territory, who would administer the laws impartially, without regard to sect or creed, for thus ordained the Constitution that governed the States as a body corporate.

The officers refused to return to the Territory, and gave up their commissions, declaring it was as much as their lives were worth to return. Politicians, who usually sought appointments with such avidity, turned coldly from all intimations that they were expected to fill the vacant posts, and for once the anomaly was known of a salaried office begging for an incumbent.

A Battalion of troops, under Col. Steptoe, a man of cool courage and energy, had been despatched to California *via*. Utah, and at this juncture lay in winter quarters at Salt Lake City. To put off the dilemma, or perchance to get rid of it entirely, the wise idea occurred to the Executive at Washington, to appoint him Governor of Utah Territory, and forward the commission to him. Should he accept, they had no fear but he would discharge the duties of the office with justice to all—and, if {411} he declined, they would gain a few months' time in which to adopt a course that would bring the difficulties of the refractory Territory to an amicable adjustment.

Meanwhile the Prophet, elated at having driven the officers from the territory, finished the additions to his harem, and went on stocking them as of old, his disciples following in his wake, and day by day plunging deeper into the crimes that outrivalled those of ancient Sodom.

After many months, when a winter had gone and spring had come, the commission of Colonel Steptoe arrived as he was raising his camp to pursue his route to California. He had dwelt for months among this heterogeneous mass of humanity, and when the office of Governor was tendered him, he peremptorily refused it, and took up his march for his distant station.

Elated still farther at Col. Steptoe's refusal, the Prophet threw off all disguise, and declared Utah independent of the Federal Government, while his adherents shouted "amen!" But the poor, deluded, and oppressed, who had been lured to that sink of pollution, who laboured from the earliest dawn to the setting sun, to fill the coffers that supported the harems, still groaned on, but less loud, for on hundreds the hand of death had been suddenly laid, how and when, their comrades knew not, they only knew they complained, and threatening to expose their oppressors, tried to escape, and were {412} found dead. The Prophet said it was a visitation from the Lord, but their comrades thought, and so expressed it among themselves, that it was rather *a visitation from the Prophet.*

Hundreds of poor labourers who, when they had been lured there, took with them their wives that they loved, none the less that the heart that was devoted to them beat under an humble garb; but, these had invariably been enticed, or when that failed, stolen from them, to stock some bashaw's den; and now, not only by hundreds but by thousands, they were deprived of the solace of a wife to welcome them when their daily toil was done, and were forced to see those they would have sacrificed life for, lengthen out the interminable length of the harem of their oppressors, while they retired to a widowed bed, doubly widowed, because she that was forever lost to him, still lived in another's arms!

Again months elapsed before the refusal of Col. Steptoe reached the Federal Government, at Washington, which brings us up to the present time. Here we find the dilemma as great as ever, for there is still no legal government in Utah Territory, and the Prophet, who lords it with a higher hand than ever,while the action of politicians at Washington remain in *statu quo.*

Also available from
GREG KOFFORD BOOKS

Re-reading Job: Understanding the Ancient World's Greatest Poem

Michael Austin

Paperback, ISBN: 978-1-58958-667-3

Job is perhaps the most difficult to understand of all books in the Bible. While a cursory reading of the text seems to relay a simple story of a righteous man whose love for God was tested through life's most difficult of challenges and rewarded for his faith through those trials, a closer reading of Job presents something far more complex and challenging. The majority of the text is a work of poetry that authors and artists through the centuries have recognized as being one of--if not the--greatest poem of the ancient world.

In *Re-reading Job: Understanding the Ancient World's Greatest Poem*, author Michael Austin shows how most readers have largely misunderstood this important work of scripture and provides insights that enable us to re-read Job in a drastically new way. In doing so, he shows that the story of Job is far more than that simple story of faith, trials, and blessings that we have all come to know, but is instead a subversive and complex work of scripture meant to inspire readers to rethink all that they thought they knew about God.

Praise for *Re-reading Job*:

"In this remarkable book, Michael Austin employs his considerable skills as a commentator to shed light on the most challenging text in the entire Hebrew Bible. Without question, readers will gain a deeper appreciation for this extraordinary ancient work through Austin's learned analysis. Rereading Job signifies that Latter-day Saints are entering a new age of mature biblical scholarship. It is an exciting time, and a thrilling work." — David Bokovoy, author, *Authoring the Old Testament*

Penny Tracts and Polemics: A Critical Analysis of Anti-Mormon Pamphleteering in Great Britain, 1837–1860

Craig L. Foster

Hardcover, ISBN: 978-1-58958-005-3

By 1860, Mormonism had enjoyed a presence in Great Britain for over twenty years. Mormon missionaries experienced unprecedented success in conversions and many new converts had left Britain's shores for a new life and a new religion in the far western mountains of the American continent.

With the success of the Mormons came tales of duplicity, priestcraft, sexual seduction, and uninhibited depravity among the new religious adherents. Thousands of pamphlets were sold or given to the British populace as a way of discouraging people from joining the Mormon Church. Foster places the creation of these English anti-Mormon pamphlets in their historical context. He discusses the authors, the impact of the publications and the Mormon response. With illustrations and detailed bibliography.

"Swell Suffering": A Biography of Maurine Whipple

Veda Tebbs Hale

Paperback, ISBN: 978-1-58958-124-1
Hardcover, ISBN: 978-1-58958-122-7

Maurine Whipple, author of what some critics consider Mormonism's greatest novel, *The Giant Joshua,* is an enigma. Her prize-winning novel has never been out of print, and its portrayal of the founding of St. George draws on her own family history to produce its unforgettable and candid portrait of plural marriage's challenges. Yet Maurine's life is full of contradictions and unanswered questions. Veda Tebbs Hale, a personal friend of the paradoxical novelist, answers these questions with sympathy and tact, nailing each insight down with thorough research in Whipple's vast but under-utilized collected papers.

Praise for *"Swell Suffering"*:

"Hale achieves an admirable balance of compassion and objectivity toward an author who seemed fated to offend those who offered to love or befriend her. . . . Readers of this biography will be reminded that Whipple was a full peer of such Utah writers as Virginia Sorensen, Fawn Brodie, and Juanita Brooks, all of whom achieved national fame for their literary and historical works during the mid-twentieth century"

—Levi S. Peterson, author of *The Backslider* and *Juanita Brooks: Mormon Historian*

Mormon Polygamous Families: Life in the Principle

Jessie L. Embry

Paperback, ISBN: 978-1-58958-098-5
Hardcover, ISBN: 978-1-58958-114-2

Mormons and non-Mormons all have their views about how polygamy was practiced in the Church of Jesus Christ of Latter-day Saints during the late nineteenth and early twentieth centuries. Embry has examined the participants themselves in order to understand how men and women living a nineteenth-century Victorian lifestyle adapted to polygamy. Based on records and oral histories with husbands, wives, and children who lived in Mormon polygamous households, this study explores the diverse experiences of individual families and stereotypes about polygamy. The interviews are in some cases the only sources of primary information on how plural families were organized. In addition, children from monogamous families who grew up during the same period were interviewed to form a comparison group. When carefully examined, most of the stereotypes about polygamous marriages do not hold true. In this work it becomes clear that Mormon polygamous families were not much different from Mormon monogamous families and non-Mormon families of the same era. Embry offers a new perspective on the Mormon practice of polygamy that enables readers to gain better understanding of Mormonism historically.

Joseph Smith's Polygamy, 3 Vols.

Brian Hales

Hardcover
Volume 1: History 978-1-58958-189-0
Volume 2: History 978-1-58958-548-5
Volume 3: Theology 978-1-58958-190-6

Perhaps the least understood part of Joseph Smith's life and teachings is his introduction of polygamy to the Saints in Nauvoo. Because of the persecution he knew it would bring, Joseph said little about it publicly and only taught it to his closest and most trusted friends and associates before his martyrdom.

In this three-volume work, Brian C. Hales provides the most comprehensive faithful examination of this much misunderstood period in LDS Church history. Drawing for the first time on every known account, Hales helps us understand the history and teachings surrounding this secretive practice and also addresses and corrects many of the numerous allegations and misrepresentations concerning it. Hales further discusses how polygamy was practiced during this time and why so many of the early Saints were willing to participate in it.

Joseph Smith's Polygamy is an essential resource in understanding this challenging and misunderstood practice of early Mormonism.

Praise for *Joseph Smith's Polygamy*:

"Brian Hales wants to face up to every question, every problem, every fear about plural marriage. His answers may not satisfy everyone, but he gives readers the relevant sources where answers, if they exist, are to be found. There has never been a more thorough examination of the polygamy idea." —Richard L. Bushman, author of *Joseph Smith: Rough Stone Rolling*

"Hales's massive and well documented three volume examination of the history and theology of Mormon plural marriage, as introduced and practiced during the life of Joseph Smith, will now be the standard against which all other treatments of this important subject will be measured." —Danel W. Bachman, author of "A Study of the Mormon Practice of Plural Marriage before the Death of Joseph Smith"

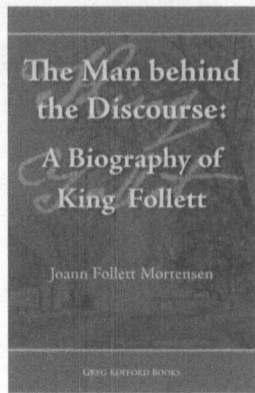

The Man behind the Discourse: A Biography of King Follett

Joann Follett Mortensen

ISBN: 978-1-58958-036-7

Who was King Follett? When he was fatally injured digging a well in Nauvoo in March 1844, why did Joseph Smith use his death to deliver the monumental doctrinal sermon now known as the King Follett Discourse? Much has been written about the sermon, but little about King.

Although King left no personal writings, Joann Follett Mortensen, King's third great-granddaughter, draws on more than thirty years of research in civic and Church records and in the journals and letters of King's peers to piece together King's story from his birth in New Hampshire and moves westward where, in Ohio, he and his wife, Louisa, made the life-shifting decision to accept the new Mormon religion.

From that point, this humble, hospitable, and hardworking family followed the Church into Missouri where their devotion to Joseph Smith was refined and burnished. King was the last Mormon prisoner in Missouri to be released from jail. According to family lore, King was one of the Prophet's bodyguards. He was also a Danite, a Mason, and an officer in the Nauvoo Legion. After his death, Louisa and their children settled in Iowa where some associated with the Cutlerities and the RLDS Church; others moved on to California. One son joined the Mormon Battalion and helped found Mormon communities in Utah, Idaho, and Arizona.

While King would have died virtually unknown had his name not been attached to the discourse, his life story reflects the reality of all those whose faith became the foundation for a new religion. His biography is more than one man's life story. It is the history of the early Restoration itself.

Dead Wood and Rushing Water: Essays on Mormon Faith, Culture, and Family

Boyd Jay Petersen

Paperback, ISBN: 978-1-58958-658-1

For over a decade, Boyd Petersen has been an active voice in Mormon studies and thought. In essays that steer a course between apologetics and criticism, striving for the balance of what Eugene England once called the "radical middle," he explores various aspects of Mormon life and culture—from the Dream Mine near Salem, Utah, to the challenges that Latter-day Saints of the millennial generation face today.

Praise for *Dead Wood and Rushing Water*:

"*Dead Wood and Rushing Water* gives us a reflective, striving, wise soul ruminating on his world. In the tradition of Eugene England, Petersen examines everything in his Mormon life from the gold plates to missions to dream mines to doubt and on to Glenn Beck, Hugh Nibley, and gender. It is a book I had trouble putting down." — Richard L. Bushman, author of *Joseph Smith: Rough Stone Rolling*

"Boyd Petersen is correct when he says that Mormons have a deep hunger for personal stories—at least when they are as thoughtful and well-crafted as the ones he shares in this collection." — Jana Riess, author of *The Twible* and *Flunking Sainthood*

"Boyd Petersen invites us all to ponder anew the verities we hold, sharing in his humility, tentativeness, and cheerful confidence that our paths will converge in the end." — Terryl. L. Givens, author of *People of Paradox: A History of Mormon Culture*

Hearken, O Ye People: The Historical Setting of Joseph Smith's Ohio Revelations

Mark Lyman Staker

Hardcover, ISBN: 978-1-58958-113-5

2010 Best Book Award - John Whitmer Historical Association

2011 Best Book Award - Mormon History Association

More of Mormonism's canonized revelations originated in or near Kirtland than any other place. Yet many of the events connected with those revelations and their 1830s historical context have faded over time. Mark Staker reconstructs the cultural experiences by which Kirtland's Latter-day Saints made sense of the revelations Joseph Smith pronounced. This volume rebuilds that exciting decade using clues from numerous archives, privately held records, museum collections, and even the soil where early members planted corn and homes. From this vast array of sources he shapes a detailed narrative of weather, religious backgrounds, dialect differences, race relations, theological discussions, food preparation, frontier violence, astronomical phenomena, and myriad daily customs of nineteenth-century life. The result is a "from the ground up" experience that today's Latter-day Saints can all but walk into and touch.

Praise for *Hearken O Ye People*:

"I am not aware of a more deeply researched and richly contextualized study of any period of Mormon church history than Mark Staker's study of Mormons in Ohio. We learn about everything from the details of Alexander Campbell's views on priesthood authority to the road conditions and weather on the four Lamanite missionaries' journey from New York to Ohio. All the Ohio revelations and even the First Vision are made to pulse with new meaning. This book sets a new standard of in-depth research in Latter-day Saint history."

-Richard Bushman, author of *Joseph Smith: Rough Stone Rolling*

"To be well-informed, any student of Latter-day Saint history and doctrine must now be acquainted with the remarkable research of Mark Staker on the important history of the church in the Kirtland, Ohio, area."

-Neal A. Maxwell Institute, Brigham Young University